THE BERNHARD FILE

AN AUNT BESSIE COLD CASE MYSTERY

DIANA XARISSA

❁ Created with Vellum

AUTHOR'S NOTE

Thank you all for your continued support of my books. I hope you all enjoyed the first book in this new series. As always, I'm really enjoying writing about Bessie and her friends.

I'm not going to repeat the same things in this note as I always do. I'm pretty sure you all know all about the books and the series.

This is a work of fiction and all of the characters are fictional creations by the author. Any resemblance they may have to any real persons, living or dead, is entirely coincidental. The businesses named throughout the book are also fictional and, again, if they resemble any real businesses, on the island or elsewhere, that is also coincidental. The historical sites mentioned within the book are all real, but the events that happen within them in the story are fictional.

Please feel free to get in touch to share your thoughts on the new series. All of my contact details are available in the back of the book.

CHAPTER 1

"It's murder this time," Andrew Cheatham told Bessie when they spoke on the telephone in the morning of the first day of November. "I'll be there next week with all of the details."

"Can't you tell me anything more now?" Elizabeth Cubbon, known as Bessie to everyone, asked.

Andrew chuckled. "I truly can't. For one thing, I have only a bare outline of the case at the moment. That would just frustrate you more. And besides, it wouldn't be fair to the others to give you the information first."

Bessie sighed. "I'm not sure joining this cold case unit was a smart idea," she grumbled. While she enjoyed working with Andrew and helping to solve cold cases, there were many aspects to the job that were frustrating, not least having to wait a month between cases.

Andrew laughed. "I'm sorry we can't meet more often. I'm doing my best, but organising the six of you isn't easy."

"Most of us are readily available," Bessie countered. Four of the members of the unit, including Bessie, lived in Laxey, after all.

"Yes, and I appreciate that the majority of the members are all in one place, but Charles and Harry and I all live in London. We're almost half of the total. It isn't just about getting the people together, though. Reviewing cases and selecting which ones we're going to consider takes time, too. Now that word is getting out about what we're doing, I've had a few people contact me to discuss cases, which means I've even more work to do in trying to find the right case for us to investigate next."

"And this time you've selected a murder case?"

"I have, and that's all I'm going to say about the case until next week, so don't even ask me any more questions."

Bessie laughed. "I wouldn't dream of it," she said, not entirely truthfully.

The pair talked briefly about Andrew's travel plans before he finally ended the conversation. "I'll be at your cottage around two on Monday, then," he told her before he put the phone down.

Bessie looked at the calendar on her wall. Next week was going to be a busy one. There was no doubt about that. Besides Andrew's visit, she had a handful of other things she needed to do as well. But there was nothing she could do at the moment, she realised with a sigh. Once Andrew arrived, she'd be busy with the cold case unit. This week would have been the perfect time to meet with other people. It was just a shame that the people with whom she wanted to meet weren't available until next week.

She'd already been for a short walk on the beach, but now that she'd spoken to Andrew, Bessie couldn't think of anything else she'd rather do than take a second one. After putting her shoes back on, she grabbed her heaviest coat and wrapped herself up warmly. A cold wind was blowing across the water, but she didn't want that to stop her from walking a good deal farther than she had earlier in the day.

After locking her cottage door, Bessie headed towards the water. Before she reached the splashing waves, she turned and began to walk along the water's edge, keeping a close eye on how far up the beach the water was actually coming. The wind rushed past her and the area felt deserted as Bessie made her way past the row of holiday cottages that had been built along the sand next to her home.

The cottages, owned by Thomas and Maggie Shimmin, were usually full all summer long with families on holiday. By November, however, they were typically unoccupied, left empty until the spring, when guests would once more return. This year was different, though. Andrew had booked the cottage closest to Bessie's for himself for a stay in November and again in December.

The other two men who would be travelling to the island for the cold case unit meeting would both be staying at the Seaview Hotel in Ramsey, one of the island's most luxurious hotels. Andrew insisted that he'd rather stay near Bessie, as the two had become good friends. He was waiting, however, to see how he fared in the cottage over the next two months before he made any arrangements for the January meeting. Bessie thought it was possible, maybe even likely, that he'd decide to move to the Seaview after spending time in December in the holiday cottage.

While her own cottage was snug and cosy in the winter months, she wasn't certain how well insulated the holiday cottages were, and she had her doubts about the heating in them, as well. She'd already told Andrew that she would understand if he decided to stay elsewhere for the weeks of the meetings early in the new year. He could move back to Laxey Beach in the spring, when the cottages would be full of holidaymakers again.

When Bessie reached the stairs to Thie yn Traie, she stopped and looked up at the mansion that was perched on the cliff above her. Originally built as a summer home for a wealthy family, the mansion was now owned by her friends George and Mary Quayle. The couple had left the island several months earlier, following a difficult murder investigation.

Bessie knew they were planning to return sometime in November. Rumour had it that their butler, Jonathan Hooper, was already back at Thie yn Traie, preparing the house for his employers. Bessie had known the man since his childhood and still thought of him as Jack, the young boy who'd fallen into the sea whenever he'd visited the beach.

Bessie could only hope that the long holiday had been good for Mary and George. Mary was quiet and shy, and Bessie thought it was likely that she'd enjoyed being away from the large social circle that George had cultivated on the island. George had been a salesman his entire adult life, selling everything from cars to insurance with great success. He was loud and boisterous and he thrived on the sorts of social gatherings that Mary hated.

No doubt George was eager to get back to the island and start filling his diary with charity dinners and other special events. After the murder of his former business associate, Bessie wasn't certain how welcome he would be, at least in some circles, but that was George's problem, not hers. She was more concerned about their daughter, Elizabeth. That was a concern for another day, though.

The wind was picking up as Bessie marched across the sand, but she was determined to keep walking for a while longer. She pushed her concerns out of her head. Now wasn't the time to worry about anything, she told herself sternly. A short while later, a row of houses came into view. The properties hadn't been there for long, and another development was being built somewhat further down the beach. The island definitely needed more housing, but Bessie rather missed being able to walk past the holiday cottages and then have the beach all to herself for miles.

Still, Hugh and Grace Watterson, Bessie's good friends, lived in one of the new houses. As she began to really feel the chill, Bessie decided that she was very happy the houses were there, after all. It took her only a minute to reach the sliding door at the back of the Wattersons' home. Through the door Bessie could see their daughter, Aalish, crawling through what appeared to be some sort of baby obstacle course that completely covered the sitting room floor. She tapped lightly on the glass.

Aalish stopped and looked over at her and then started to babble loudly. Grace rushed out of the kitchen and crossed to Bessie.

"Hello, hello," she said brightly. "Come in and ignore the baby. She's just making noise because she can." Grace was a pretty blonde. Today she was wearing jeans and a sweatshirt, her hair caught back in a low ponytail.

Bessie grinned at her. "Hello. I was walking past and I thought it might be nice to warm up for a bit."

"I'll put the kettle on," Grace replied.

As Grace returned to the kitchen, Aalish stopped making noise and began to attempt to crawl through a small tunnel. There was just a slight incline for her to negotiate, and Bessie watched, fascinated, as Aalish struggled to make it up the small slope. Every time she moved forward a few inches, she'd find herself sliding backwards. The first time she giggled as she went, but by the third attempt, she seemed to be getting angry.

Bessie took off her coat and then crossed to the island that separated the kitchen from the sitting room. "She's getting mad with that tunnel," she told Grace.

"She gets really frustrated with it," Grace agreed. "The other side has rows of bumps so it's a lot easier for her to crawl up, but she hasn't worked out the difference yet, so she keeps trying the smooth side and can't manage it."

Aalish let out a loud yell and then turned her back on the tunnel and began to crawl away. She stopped in front of a huge pile of cuddly toys and, after some complicated-looking maneuvers, managed to end up sitting next to them. Grace laughed as her daughter began to pick up toys and then toss them away.

"She's looking for her favourite," she told Bessie. "I keep hiding him at the bottom of the pile. She's really starting to understand object permanence. She knows Mr. Squishy is in there somewhere."

"Mr. Squishy?"

Grace blushed. "Hugh named him," she said quickly.

Bessie laughed. "Aalish may give him a different name once she's talking."

"I certainly hope so, although, to be fair, he is very squishy."

A happy squeal drew Bessie's attention. Aalish was hugging a small blue bear, a beaming smile on her face.

"I'm going to guess that's Mr. Squishy," Bessie said.

"It is. And when Aalish goes for her nap, Mr. Squishy is going for a swim in the washing machine."

"I didn't think you could put cuddly toys in the washing machine."

"This one is definitely machine washable. It said so on the tag. Mr. Squishy gets a lot of love, so he gets washed pretty regularly. Most of the others just get thrown around."

Back on the floor, Aalish had decided it was time to move again. She got down on all fours and then started to try to crawl, still holding on tightly to Mr. Squishy. That made crawling difficult, of course, and the cuddly toys that were now scattered everywhere didn't help.

"Tears in five, four, three, two..." Grace muttered as her

daughter struggled to move, one hand pulling on Mr. Squishy while his leg was trapped under her own knee. When the angry shouts began, Grace went over and picked Aalish up off the floor.

"Time for a snuggle," she told the baby, "and maybe a biscuit?"

Bessie sipped her tea as Grace gave Aalish a treat. "How are you?" she asked the girl as Grace took a drink from her own mug.

"I'm fine. Actually, I'm really good. With everything that Hugh is busy doing, we've decided that I shouldn't go back to work until at least September. Now that Aalish is getting bigger, I'm really enjoying spending time with her, too. I've joined a few Mums and Tots groups, and we have a regular schedule of activities at gyms, the pool, and playgrounds around the island. It keeps Aalish busy, and talking to other mums keeps me from going mad."

Grace had been a primary school teacher in Douglas when she'd met Hugh, a constable with the Laxey constabulary. As Bessie had never had children of her own, over the years she'd acted as something of an honorary aunt to the boys and girls of Laxey, giving them treats when they were playing on the beach and offering them a place to go if they needed to get away from parents who didn't seem to understand them. Hugh had had a difficult childhood. His parents had a long list of expectations for their only child, but, when he'd still been quite young, Hugh had decided he wanted to join the police.

Regular fights about his future had driven Hugh to spend quite a few nights during his teen years at Bessie's. Hugh was in his mid-twenties now, and both Bessie and his parents were incredibly proud of the young man he'd become. His parents thought Grace was wonderful and they doted on little Aalish. They were also pleased that Hugh had recently gone back to school. He was hoping to earn a university degree so that one day he could be promoted to inspector. In addition to working full-time for the constabulary and going to school, Hugh was part of Andrew's cold case unit.

"He isn't trying to do too much, is he?" Bessie asked. "I'd hate to think that he's too busy to spend time with Aalish."

"He's doing a lot, but so far it's not been too bad. His classes are only a few nights a week and he manages to do most of his homework during his lunch break at work. The cold case unit wasn't too much extra work last month. I hope that won't change. John's been very good about giving him Saturdays off, so he usually spends nearly the whole day with Aalish and me. He's been talking about taking Aalish to the park without me one of these days, as well."

"You don't sound enthusiastic," Bessie told her.

Grace shrugged. "I hate being away from her," she said, pulling the baby into a hug. Aalish, who was gnawing on her hard biscuit, let out a shout of protest. Grace laughed. "Yes, I know, you're eating and I'm interrupting. You're already growing far too independent for my liking."

"I believe it only gets worse from here," Bessie told her.

"I know. She isn't even walking yet, although she does seem to get into everything anyway. She'll be a year old next month. That doesn't seem possible." Grace hesitated and then flushed. "It's terrible timing, but Hugh and I have been talking about having another baby."

"No doubt that's a difficult thing to decide," Bessie said. Having never married, it wasn't something she'd ever had to consider.

"After I had Aalish, I said I didn't want any more, at least not until she was in school, but I don't know. I miss my tiny, toothless baby."

Aalish chose that moment to throw what was left of her biscuit. Bessie was certain Aalish hadn't aimed it at her, but the half-chewed and rather soggy lump landed neatly on Bessie's lap.

"Oh, goodness, I'm so sorry," Grace exclaimed as Aalish began to yell as she tried to wriggle her way out of her mother's arms.

"It's fine," Bessie told her, using a paper napkin to carefully pick up the biscuit remains. Soggy crumbs clung to her trousers, but Bessie opted to leave them where they were, rather than risk rubbing them into the fabric. Once they'd dried, they would be easy to remove, she told herself.

Grace carried Aalish to the sink and washed her hands and face, all while Aalish screamed as if she were in great pain. When Grace put her back on the floor, Aalish made a beeline to Mr. Squishy. It was only when she had the bear back in her grasp that she stopped crying.

"I don't know how you do it," Bessie told Grace honestly.

"There are days when I'm not sure I'm going to make it until Hugh gets home. On those days, I don't want any more children, ever. But then, there are days when she's just amazing and I feel as if I want to fill up the house with dozens more beautiful babies."

"Dozens?"

Grace laughed. "Okay, maybe not dozens. We can't afford dozens, not on a police constable's salary, anyway. The extra money from the cold case unit is the real reason why I'm not rushing back to work."

They weren't being paid much for being a part of the unit, but it was the first time in her life that Bessie had ever been paid for work. An inheritance at eighteen had given her enough money to buy her tiny cottage so that she could move out of her parents' house. Wise investments by her advocate, Doncan Quayle, had kept her from having to find employment once she'd been settled in her new home. Thanks to Doncan, and, later, his son, Bessie now had a considerable amount of money in the bank. She was able to live quite comfortably in the cottage that she'd had extended twice during her years there. The money she was receiving for her part in the cold case unit was simply being added to her bank balance, although Bessie had plans to donate the unexpected income to charity on a regular basis.

"Andrew will be back next week," Bessie said after a moment.

"Yes, Hugh is looking forward to another case. He's hoping for murder this time."

"I spoke to Andrew earlier today and he confirmed that it will be murder this time."

"Well, Hugh will be happy to hear that, anyway."

"You aren't?"

"I just find murder cases quite sad. I'm glad you and the rest of the unit are trying to solve old cases, but it always upsets me to hear about people killing other people. Not that Hugh tells me anything about the cases you're discussing," Grace added quickly.

"I'm just hoping we'll be able to solve the case," Bessie told her. "Andrew didn't think we'd able to solve more than a single case in a year, and we solved the very first one. I hate the idea of leaving a murderer out there, unpunished."

Grace shivered and looked at Aalish. "You are never moving out of this house, young lady," she said sternly.

Aalish looked up and then waved Mr. Squishy at them. "Babbbbaaabbbaaaa," she replied.

"Somehow I don't think that was a yes," Bessie said.

Grace frowned. "Maybe I don't want any more children. Just keeping one safe is going to be difficult enough."

Aalish had continued to wave her toy in the air. Now it flew out of her hand across the room. Aalish stared after it and then began to sob. Grace jumped up and made her way through the piles of toys and playthings. When she held out the bear to Aalish a moment later, the little girl stared at it and then turned and crawled away.

"Oh, dear. She's mad at him for flying away," Bessie said, trying not to laugh.

"She was the one who threw him," Grace sighed. She dropped the toy on top of the plastic tunnel and then looked at the clock.

"You have to be somewhere," Bessie guessed, getting to her feet.

"We're having lunch with some friends," Grace replied. "We've plenty of time, though. You don't need to rush away."

Bessie shook her head. "It's later than I'd realised. I need to get home and...." She paused. There wasn't really any reason for her to rush home, but she knew Grace had things to do. Aalish picked that moment to crawl into a wall. As she began to cry, Bessie pulled her coat back around her.

"It was lovely to see you, anyway," she told Grace, who was rocking the sobbing child.

"Please, visit any time," Grace told her as she followed her to the door.

Once Bessie had exited the house, the air felt refreshing, at least for the first few minutes. Having had a short rest, she set off at a rapid pace. Just past the stairs to Thie yn Traie, she stopped in her tracks. The holiday cottages were all supposed to be empty, but the sliding door to the last cottage was noticeably ajar.

CHAPTER 2

"*H*ello?" Bessie called, taking a step closer to the cottage. *Surely either Maggie or Thomas must be in there taking care of some job that needs doing*, she thought. "Hello? Maggie? Thomas?"

Her words seemed to echo around her. After everything that had happened on the island in the past three years, Bessie now never left home without her mobile phone. As she pulled it out, she tried to decide whom to ring first. She didn't want to ring the police if Maggie or Thomas were in the cottage somewhere and simply couldn't hear her. But what if they were both tucked up at home on this cold and blustery day? If they were, then the police needed to be rung. As the wind blew harder, she pressed one on her speed dial.

"Hello?"

"Doona? It's Bessie. I'm standing on the beach behind the last holiday cottage. The sliding door is ajar."

Doona sighed. "Don't go inside."

"I have no intention of going inside. Maggie or Thomas may be in there, actually, but I shouted and no one has replied."

"I'll be there as soon as I can and I'll bring John with me. He's not working today and he's sitting right here."

Bessie could hear John's voice in the background. "Keep her on the phone," he told Doona. "And tell her to put some distance between herself and the cottage, but to keep an eye on that door. I'll have a constable there in five minutes or less."

"Did you hear all of that?" Doona asked Bessie.

"I did, yes, but it may be nothing."

"And it may be something. I'm going to hand you over to John so that I can comb my hair and find some shoes. Here you go."

"I've rung the station and asked for the nearest constable," John told her. "He or she should be there in just a minute or two."

"I should have rung Maggie first," Bessie sighed. "She may be in the cottage, working."

"I'll ring her once I give Doona her phone back. For now, is there anyone else around?"

Bessie looked up and down the beach. "Aside from a few seagulls, I'm alone."

John sighed. "And Andrew doesn't arrive until Monday."

"He has a murder case for us this time," Bessie replied.

Police Inspector John Rockwell was in charge of the Laxey Constabulary. He'd moved to the island just a short time before Bessie had stumbled across her first dead body, right on this beach. The pair had become friends in the months that had followed, as Bessie had found herself involved in even more murder investigations. Now they were colleagues on the cold case unit, something Bessie never could have imagined when she'd first met the man.

"Let's hope we don't have a murder case for him," John replied. "I'm giving you back to Doona. We're on our way."

Bessie nodded and then frowned at herself. Obviously, John couldn't see her nodding.

"So how are you?" Doona asked a moment later.

"I'm fine. I took a short walk this morning and then, after I spoke to Andrew, I took a longer one."

"How is Andrew?"

"He's looking forward to being here next week. He's bringing us a murder case this time."

Doona Moore was Bessie's closest friend. When they'd met in a Manx language class, Doona had just started a job as a civilian receptionist at the Laxey Constabulary. She'd moved to Laxey to try to start over again after her second marriage had failed. Bessie had done what she could to help her new friend through that very difficult period, and the two had grown even closer in the years since. Doona was the fourth member of the cold case unit who lived on the Isle of Man.

"It would be very satisfying to solve this one, too," Doona said.

"I'd quite like to solve them all, but Andrew doesn't think that's possible."

"He should have more faith in you."

"In all of us."

"Hello?"

Bessie jumped and nearly dropped her phone. "There's a constable here," she told Doona. "It's Constable Stone."

"We're only a minute or two away. I'm going to end the call. We'll see you very soon," Doona replied.

Bessie pushed the button to break the connection and then dropped her phone back into her pocket. "Good morning," she greeted the young constable.

"Is it still morning?" he asked.

A glance at her watch showed Bessie that it was just a

handful of minutes before midday. "It's later than I'd realised," she sighed. "No wonder I'm so hungry."

The man nodded. "I was just going on my lunch break when I got this call."

"I am sorry. I don't mean to be a bother."

He smiled at her. "No one would ever accuse you of being a bother," he assured her. "But what's wrong? I was just told to get down to Laxey Beach and look for Aunt Bessie."

"The door is ajar," Bessie told him, gesturing towards the cottage in front of her.

He sighed. "This cottage is nothing but trouble. I'm sure we talked about it the last time I spoke with you."

Bessie nodded. She'd met the young man only once before, but they'd had time for a lengthy chat. During that conversation, he'd mentioned that he'd frequently been dispatched to this cottage during the brief period when Thomas and Maggie had tried putting a security system in it. They'd given up after several false alarms that the alarm company had insisted on blaming on the wind.

"The owners are trying to get planning permission to tear it down and replace it," Bessie told him. "Thus far, they haven't managed it." There was nothing to stop them tearing it down, but Maggie had told Bessie that they weren't prepared to go to the expense of doing that until they were certain they could replace it with a new cottage.

"I'm sure I heard some stories about it, but I can't remember them now. It looks to be the same as all of the other cottages. Why tear it down?"

"There was a tragic accident here not long after the cottages were built. Since then, there have been two murders in the cottage, as well. Apparently, holidaymakers are reluctant to stay in a cottage where someone had been murdered."

The constable shuddered. "I don't blame them."

"But how are you?" Bessie asked. When she'd met the

man, she'd been convinced that something had been bothering him, but she'd been at the centre of a murder investigation and hadn't had the time to really get to know him.

"I'm fine," he replied, turning and staring out at the sea.

"You were going to come back for tea again and you never did," Bessie reminded him. "The invitation is still open."

He looked over at her and then nodded slowly. "I'd like that," he said softly. "I could do with…"

"We're here," Doona's voice carried across the beach.

Bessie watched as her friend rushed through the sand towards her. Doona was in her mid-forties. Her hair was brown with blonde highlights, and Bessie thought it looked as if it had been cut and styled quite recently. Today she was wearing glasses, a pair that Bessie had never seen before, although she typically wore coloured contact lenses that gave her bright green eyes.

When she reached Bessie, she pulled her into a hug. "I can't believe I haven't seen you in over a fortnight," she said as she released her. "I'm busy with the kids and John, but that's no excuse for neglecting my dearest friend."

"I haven't felt at all neglected," Bessie assured her. "I do understand how busy you are."

After a long and difficult journey, Doona and John Rockwell were now in a relationship of some sort. The last Bessie had heard, neither of them were interested in defining it more clearly. John had been married when he'd first moved to the island. He'd been through a difficult divorce and the subsequent, unexpected death of his former wife, Sue. Her death had left him to bring up their two teenaged children on his own. Bessie was pleased that he now had Doona to help with Thomas and Amy, and she knew that her friend was crazy about the man and the children.

Having lived on her own for more years than Doona had

been alive, Bessie truly hadn't minded not seeing Doona for a few weeks. Now, however, as Doona hugged her again, she realised she had missed her friend.

"But where's John?" Bessie asked as she looked back down the beach.

"He's waiting in the car park for Thomas and Maggie," Doona told her. "He rang them on the drive here. They're on their way."

Bessie sighed and then turned and looked at the cottage again. "I was really hoping they were in there, doing something," she said.

"That's what John was hoping as well," Doona replied. "Here they are."

Bessie watched as John escorted the couple across the sand. Maggie looked mad at the world as she stomped along behind John. Thomas had spent a large part of the previous year unwell, and he was still considerably thinner than he had been formerly. They were halfway to the cottage when Thomas stopped and began to cough. It was at least a minute before the coughing spell ended.

"Sorry about that," Thomas said, his voice drifting across the sand as they restarted their progress towards Bessie and the others.

"I told you to stay home," Maggie snapped.

"I wasn't about to leave you to face this on your own," Thomas replied. "We've no idea what the police are going to find in that cottage."

"It was Bessie who found the door ajar," Maggie said sharply. "No doubt there's a dead man in the sitting room or a dead woman in the bathtub."

Bessie frowned. While she had found more than her fair share of dead bodies in the past few years, she'd never gone looking for them, and she resented the implication that she was in some way responsible for them.

"Let's not jump to any conclusions," John said as he came up behind the couple. "There could be any number of reasons why the door is open."

"Clearly, someone broke into the cottage yet again," Maggie said angrily. "I don't understand why, but this cottage seems to be the island's most popular spot for break-ins."

"We do our best to keep an eye on the cottages down here," John told her. "But they're hidden from the road, and I can't make a constable walk up and down the beach all night long."

Bessie thought John looked tired. In his mid-forties, John had dark hair and brilliant green eyes. He was movie-star handsome, at least in Bessie's opinion. During his difficult divorce, he'd lost more weight than had been good for him. He'd regained most of it, and then Sue had fallen ill. Her long illness had taken another toll on John, but in the months since then, he'd been doing better. Now Bessie wondered if there was something else wrong, something about which she knew nothing.

Maggie opened her mouth to reply, but Thomas held up a hand. "We greatly appreciate everything that you do," he told John. "It was our decision to build the cottages here, and one of the main reasons they appeal to our guests is that they are off the beaten path to some extent. We've taken all of the furniture out of this cottage. There's nothing in there but bare walls. I can't imagine why anyone would want to break in, not when the other cottages are furnished."

"I suspect it's the most likely target because it's the last one. There's nothing past it except for empty beach," John said. "If you've nowhere to stay for the night, even an empty cottage is better than sleeping outside."

"Are you going to go in and see what Bessie's found, then?" Maggie demanded. "The sooner you start investigating the murder, the better."

John glanced at Bessie, who frowned. She opened her mouth to reply, but he slowly shook his head.

"I'm just waiting to get word that there are constables in place at the front of the cottage," John told Maggie. "If there is someone inside, I don't want him or her going out the front door as I go in the back."

Maggie nodded. "I hope you catch whoever it is and lock them up for a very long time. Not that catching one person will stop the next half-dozen who want to break in here. Maybe we should tear this cottage down, regardless of whether we can get planning permission to replace it or not."

"It's a large expense that we don't need to incur right now," Thomas said softly.

"And now the cottage is going to be a crime scene again, anyway," Maggie said gloomily. "We won't even be able to go inside for weeks."

John's mobile buzzed. He glanced at the screen and then looked over at Constable Stone. "I'm going inside. You stay out here, and if anyone comes out, stop them."

The constable nodded. "Yes, sir," he said smartly.

John took a few steps forward. The constable followed, with Maggie on his heels. Bessie glanced at Doona, and then they also took a few steps closer to the cottage.

"It's a parade," Thomas muttered as he fell into step behind Bessie.

She looked over at him and shrugged. They all took a few more steps, and then John stopped.

"You all need to wait here," he said.

"You aren't going in alone," Doona said. "You've no idea who could be in there."

"I have backup all around the cottage," he replied.

"You need backup in the cottage," she argued. "Ideally, a dozen of your strongest men."

John chuckled. "I know you worry about me, but this is my job, one I've been doing for many years."

Doona nodded. "Just take someone else in with you, please? Even one other person would make me feel a lot better."

Sighing, John pulled out his mobile and typed something. A moment later, a uniformed constable appeared from around the side of the cottage.

"We're going inside," John told the young man, one whom Bessie didn't recognise.

"Yes, sir," he replied, looking uncertain.

"Wait here," John told Bessie and the others.

As he walked up the steps to the sliding door, he put on gloves and then handed a pair to the constable. "Hello?" he shouted through the open door. "Is anyone here?"

It felt to Bessie as if everyone on the beach stopped breathing. They stood together, all seemingly straining to listen for noises from within the cottage.

"Police," John said loudly after a moment. "We're coming inside."

He reached out and slid the door open the rest of the way. It squeaked noisily as he pushed it, sticking a handful of times along the track.

"Police," John said again, before he slowly stepped into the cottage.

Doona inhaled sharply and then turned around. "I should have stayed at home," she muttered.

Bessie patted her friend's arm. "John will be fine. It's probably nothing. Maybe the wind blew the door open."

She knew better, and so did Doona, but the words were enough to distract Doona for a moment or two as John disappeared from view. The constable followed him, and the group on the beach fell silent. Bessie couldn't tear her eyes away from the door through which the two men had gone.

"How long can it take to go through an empty cottage?" Maggie snapped a minute or two later. "They should be able to tell at a glance whether there are any bodies anywhere."

"The bedrooms have built-in wardrobes, don't they?" Bessie asked. "It will take them a while to open and check all of them."

"We should take off all of the doors," Maggie told Thomas. "All of the doors between the rooms as well as the doors to the wardrobes. That would make it harder for people to hide inside."

Thomas nodded. "And we could use the doors to replace damaged ones from the other cottages. We should have thought of that before."

"Doors get damaged in the cottages?" Doona asked. "How do you damage a door?"

Maggie sighed. "I do believe some of our guests do it for sport. We had one incident last year when a family of four managed to damage three doors in one week."

"What happened to the doors?" Bessie asked.

"I've no idea," Maggie replied. "All I know for certain is that after they'd left, when I inspected the property, three of the doors had holes in them."

"My goodness," Bessie exclaimed.

"Arc they terribly costly to replace?" Doona wondered.

"Obviously, we don't have the very best quality interior doors that are available, but there was still an expense involved in replacing them," Maggie told her.

"I hope you made the guests pay for them," Doona said.

"Oh, aye. We require a deposit and fortunately, it was enough to cover the replacement doors. We've increased the amount we take as a deposit now, though, as the old amount was only just enough to replace those three doors," Maggie said.

Doona opened her mouth to reply, but stopped as John

appeared in the doorway. He stepped out of the cottage with a frown on his face.

"Please tell me you didn't find any dead men," Maggie said as she walked towards the man.

"We didn't find any dead men," John told her.

"What about women?" Maggie asked. "Children? Dogs? Cats? Horses? What's in there?"

"We didn't find anything," John told her as the constable followed him out of the building.

"Nothing?" Maggie demanded. "What does that mean?"

"It means that the cottage is completely empty. We didn't find any evidence that anyone has been inside, either. All of the doors were standing open and every room looked as if it hadn't been touched in weeks or even months," John replied.

"I was in there just last week," Maggie argued.

John shrugged. "I'd like you to take a walk through the building with me now. Maybe you'll notice something I missed. In the meantime, Constable Stone, can you please see if you can get any fingerprints from the sliding door?"

The constable nodded, but with a frown on his face. As John walked away, he looked at Bessie. "There's no way I'm going to be able to get any good prints from that door," he told her.

He was still trying when Maggie and John returned from their inspection of the cottage's interior.

"Nothing," Maggie said to Thomas. "It looks exactly the same as it did last week when I dusted and vacuumed. Nothing has changed."

"Did you use the sliding door at all on that visit?" John asked.

Maggie shook her head. "I parked in the car park and walked from there to the front door. After I cleaned, I went back out the front door."

"Where do you keep the vacuum?" Bessie asked.

Maggie looked surprised and then nodded at the cottage. "In the storage cupboard between the bedrooms," she said.

"So the cottage isn't completely empty," Bessie said thoughtfully. "What else is in that cupboard?"

"Just the supplies I need to keep the cottage clean. There's no point in dragging such things from cottage to cottage. We keep a cupboard of supplies in every cottage, but it's kept locked at all times," Maggie told her.

"So your guests can't clean up after themselves?" Bessie asked.

"As if they would," Maggie shot back.

Maybe they would if they had cleaning supplies, Bessie thought. She looked over at Thomas, and he winked at her.

"And nothing has been moved in the storage cupboard?" Bessie asked.

"That door was locked when I went through," John told her. "Maggie checked, though."

"I suppose it's possible that the bottle of glass cleaner might have been moved an inch or two or something," Maggie said. "Nothing is missing, though."

Bessie nodded as she tried to think. Someone must have been in the cottage, but why?

John was busy on his mobile. After a moment, he looked up. "Maggie, if you're satisfied that nothing is amiss, I'll just check that the door is secure and be on my way."

Maggie nodded. She slid the door shut with a bang and then turned the key in the lock. When she stepped back, John tested the door.

"All secure," he said.

"And much ado about nothing," Maggie muttered as she spun around and began to march back down the beach towards the car park.

"Thank you," Thomas said to John before he rushed after his wife.

"I am sorry…" Bessie began, but John held up a hand.

"You've nothing to be sorry about," he told her. "You did the right thing, ringing me, or rather, ringing Doona. There could have been something seriously wrong. I'm just glad it turned out to be a false alarm."

"I'm going to keep a close eye on this cottage for the next week," Bessie told him.

"And then Andrew will be here," Doona said. "He'll be able to watch over things for a while after that."

Bessie nodded. Andrew had been an inspector with Scotland Yard. She knew both she and Maggie would sleep better once he'd arrived on the island, especially since he'd be staying at a cottage on the beach.

CHAPTER 3

*D*oona and John walked Bessie back to her cottage.
"I'll just have a quick walk through the cottage
before we go," Doona told Bessie at the cottage door.

"There's no need for you to do any such thing," Bessie
protested.

"But you'll let me anyway, because you don't want me to
worry about you," Doona replied.

Bessie frowned. "John doesn't fuss," she pointed out.

Doona laughed. "He'd go through the cottage if I didn't."

Bessie looked at John, who nodded. She sighed, but didn't
argue any further. While she hated being fussed over, it still
hadn't been all that long since someone had broken into her
cottage. Although all the perpetrator had done was make a
huge mess, Bessie found herself worrying every time she left
the cottage for any length of time. Now she stood in the
small kitchen with John while Doona walked around on the
floor above them.

"I wish she wouldn't fuss so much," Bessie sighed.

"Even though nothing was disturbed, I suspect someone
broke into that last cottage," John said seriously. "Whoever it

was may have simply been looking for a warm and dry place to stay, but he or she may have been looking for things to steal. If that's the case, the person may try again at one of the other cottages along the beach, which includes yours."

"I've nothing worth stealing."

"You have some lovely antique furniture, but regardless, a thief wouldn't be able to tell what's in here without breaking in."

Bessie frowned. "There are several other cottages between here and there. They've no reason to break into mine."

"I know you would have rung us if the sliding door had been ajar when you'd first set out on your walk," John said. "I don't suppose you specifically noticed that it was shut, did you?"

"I should have thought of that," Bessie said, closing her eyes and trying to think. After a moment, she shook her head. "I was watching the water on my way out," she told him. "The tide was coming in and I was walking right at the water's edge. I didn't look up at the cottages at all."

"I'd assumed as much, but I wanted to be certain. I suspect the break-in happened overnight, but that's just speculation."

"The door was definitely not open yesterday afternoon," Bessie told him. "I took a walk around four o'clock and I definitely remember looking at that last cottage as I went."

"Why do you remember it so clearly?"

"There were footprints in the sand near the cottage," Bessie told him. "When I saw them, I looked up at the cottage to check that it was secure."

"Footprints? You should have rung me."

"It isn't all that unusual. People sometimes park in the car park for the cottages and walk their dogs on the beach. The people who live in the new houses sometimes walk up this way as well. Thomas and Maggie are down here at least a few times each week, too. Although I rarely see anyone on the beach at this time of the year, I often see footprints."

"And yesterday you saw some around the last cottage?"

"They were between the cottage and the sea. They didn't actually go all the way up to the sliding door, though. It looked as if someone walked from the car park down to the beach and then back again, with a small detour to walk behind the cottage, but whoever it was stayed several feet away from the back of the building."

John nodded and then pulled out a notebook and made a few notes. "If you see footprints again, I want you to let me know," he said as he slid his notebook back into his pocket. "I'm going to ask Maggie and Thomas to do the same."

"Except they'll be reporting my prints and I'll be reporting theirs," Bessie suggested.

"I'd rather have that than miss something important," John replied.

Bessie might have argued further, but Doona interrupted.

"Sorry I took so long," she said in the doorway. "Bessie, I want to borrow the book on your bedside table when you've finished it."

Bessie laughed. "The cover is very eye-catching, isn't it?"

"I saw it as I walked into the room, and I had to read the back cover. Then I had to read the first few pages. If I hadn't known that John was waiting for me, I'd have read a lot more," she replied.

"I've nearly finished it, and I hate to say it, but I think the cover is the best part of the book. It's been quite disappointing."

Doona frowned. "The first chapter was gripping."

"I felt that it went downhill from there, but you may not agree. If I don't see you before Tuesday, I'll bring it to the first cold case unit meeting. I know I'll be finished with it by then."

"Thanks, I think."

Bessie gave them each a hug and then let them out of the cottage. After she'd watched them drive away, she glanced at the sign right outside the door. "Treoghe Bwaane" meant "Widow's Cottage" in Manx, the island's native language. The sign had already been in place when Bessie had purchased the cottage, but she'd felt it was the perfect name for what she'd believed would be only her temporary home.

Her childhood had been spent in the US, even though she'd been born on the island. When she'd been seventeen, her parents had chosen to return to the island and had insisted that Bessie accompany them. She'd been forced to leave behind the man she loved. Matthew Saunders had attempted to follow her some months later, but had perished during the lengthy sea journey. He'd left everything he owned to Bessie, providing her with an inheritance that allowed her to buy her cottage and live independently.

The cottage was small and cosy, even after two additions, and Bessie couldn't imagine calling anywhere else home. She'd been there for more years than she wanted to consider, having stopped counting birthdays once she'd received her free bus pass at sixty. There seemed little point in worrying about the ones that came after that, at least until it was time to receive a birthday card from the Queen, which wouldn't happen until she'd reached one hundred. Vaguely aware that she was around halfway between those two milestones, Bessie preferred to think of herself as being in the later years of middle age.

* * *

THE REST of the week seemed to rush past. Bessie finished the book that Doona wanted to borrow and met her friend for lunch one day to pass it along. Although Thanksgiving wasn't celebrated on the island, Bessie still enjoyed marking the day with a special dinner. She spent some hours one afternoon working through some preliminary plans for the day, but not actually booking anything. Instead, she wanted to use the event as an excuse for contacting someone the following week.

She also spent some time working with Mark Blake, Manx National Heritage's head of special projects. Christmas at the Castle was a huge fundraiser at Castle Rushen and it took a great deal of organising. Bessie was more than happy to help for the third year in a row, but when they met, she warned Mark that she was somewhat busier than normal. Andrew had asked her not to tell anyone about the cold case unit, hoping to avoid any press coverage of what they were doing, so she could make only vague excuses about spending time with Andrew, who was planning on visiting regularly.

And every day she walked on the beach and, during every walk, she found herself staring at the last cottage. It always appeared deserted, the sliding door tightly shut. As for footprints, she saw only a few of those, and in every instance she was able to identify who'd left them. In spite of that, she rang John every day and reported what she'd seen, which was nearly always evidence of either Thomas or Maggie working on the cottages.

By Monday, Bessie was more than ready for Andrew to arrive. John had agreed that she could stop worrying about footprints in the sand while Andrew was visiting, and Bessie was looking forward to seeing the man, who'd become a close friend over the past few years. They'd met in the middle of a murder investigation in the UK, and Andrew had visited the island on several occasions since. When he'd first mentioned the cold case unit, Bessie hadn't been certain how she felt about the idea, and now, even after the first case had been solved, she still hadn't decided. Perhaps this second case, a murder investigation, would help her make up her mind.

On Monday morning, she took an extra-long walk on the beach. When she got home, she picked up her telephone. She'd wanted to speak to Andy Caine for quite some time, but she hadn't managed it. Andy had spent a large portion of his teen years in Bessie's spare bedroom, another young man with a difficult family life. He was now in his mid-twenties. A few years earlier, he'd come into a completely unexpected inheritance that had allowed him to chase his dream of becoming a chef and owning his own restaurant. He'd spent nearly two years at culinary school in the UK and then returned to the island, determined to start his business.

Instead, he'd found himself in great demand catering parties and events for the island's first-ever party planner, Elizabeth Quayle. Elizabeth was George and Mary Quayle's only daughter. She had dropped out of several universities, unable to work out what she wanted to do with her life. Her parents provided her with a luxurious lifestyle, and Bessie had been pleasantly surprised when the girl had proven to be a very hard worker once she'd started her own business. As well as establishing a professional relationship, Elizabeth and Andy soon developed a personal one as well.

While Elizabeth's business had thrived, Andy had found himself unable to find the perfect location for his restaurant. He'd continued to live with his mother in the same small cottage where she'd lived for her entire life. Bessie had grown somewhat frustrated with the man, mostly because she was eager for him to open the restaurant that she knew was going to be a huge success. Andy was a brilliant chef and especially excelled at puddings, something Bessie loved.

Some seven months previously, after a murder case that had upset just about everyone on the island, George and Mary had gone on an extended holiday, and Elizabeth had gone with them. While they'd been gone, Andy had begun catering events for Jennifer Johnson, one of the two new party planners who'd started businesses on the island as soon as had Elizabeth left. Bessie had heard quite a few things about Jennifer that concerned her, but when she'd rung Andy to discuss them with him, she'd discovered that he'd gone to Paris to take a class. He had been expected back on the island on Sunday, and Bessie wasn't going to wait any longer to try to reach him.

"Hello?"

"Anne? It's Bessie. Is Andy back on the island yet?"

Anne was Andy's mother, and she knew how eager Bessie was to speak to her son. "He got back on the late ferry last night. He's still in bed. I'll have him ring you when he's up."

"I'd appreciate that."

"Actually, I should say that I'll add you to the list, as at least a half dozen people have rung so far this morning," Anne added.

"Really? He should be flattered to be so popular."

Anne laughed. "I'm not sure popular is the right word. His estate agent wants to show him more houses, hoping he'll finally buy something. Three different people have rung to ask him to consider coming to work for them as a private chef. Two restaurant managers have rung to offer him jobs in their kitchens. Jennifer Johnson has rung to see if he can cater a dozen parties in the next week or two. And Elizabeth Quayle rang."

"Did she, now? What did she want?"

"She didn't say. She simply asked me to tell Andy that she'd rung."

"Surely she has his mobile number," Bessie said, more to herself than to Anne.

"Of course she does. I wish I knew what was happening with those two."

"Yes, well, please add me to the list," Bessie told her.

"I will. If he isn't up soon, I'm going to start making a racket."

Bessie laughed. "Good luck."

With that chore out of the way, at least for the time being, Bessie grabbed a book from the nearest bookshelf and settled in to read. Her stomach rumbled loudly some hours later. She made herself a bowl of soup and some toast, turning pages as she worked. Just after two, she found herself being interrupted by a knock on the door.

"Andrew, hello," she said, feeling slightly disconcerted by the need to drag herself back to reality.

"I feel as if I've interrupted something," he said, glancing behind her.

"I was just reading," Bessie explained. "It's a book I've read before, but I can't for the life of me remember who was responsible for the murder. I seem to recall some sort of twist in the end, but I could be mistaken. Regardless, the writing is excellent and I was quite lost in the pages."

"Perhaps I should go away and come back later."

Bessie actually gave the idea some thought before shaking her head. "It's fine. The book will wait for me. You're only here for a fortnight."

"And I'd really like to start my stay with a long walk on the beach," he told her. "You don't have to join me if you'd rather read."

"Even though I'm enjoying the book, I very rarely turn down a chance to walk on the beach," she replied.

A short while later, they were walking along the sand, heading towards the stairs to Thie yn Traie.

"This cottage has been causing more trouble, I hear," he said, stopping behind the last cottage.

Bessie nodded. "The sliding door was ajar one day recently. The police came, but they didn't find anything."

"I shall have to keep a close eye on all of the cottages while I'm here."

They walked a bit further before Andrew spoke again. "I believe the Quayles will be back around the same time as I leave," he said as they passed the stairs to Thie yn Traie.

Bessie wondered about the source of his information, but she didn't ask. The man worked for Scotland Yard, after all. He was officially retired, but the cold case unit was being run under their supervision.

"It will be nice to have them back on the island," she said after a moment.

They chatted about Andrew's family as they walked for a while longer. He had children, grandchildren, and great-grandchildren, so he always had a number of stories to share with Bessie. When he was done, she brought him up to date on recent events on the island. The wind was starting to pick up as they got back to Bessie's cottage.

"I need to check that Charles and Harry arrived safely," he told her at her door. "I'll be back around five to take you somewhere nice for dinner. I thought maybe we could go into Douglas for a change."

"That sounds good," Bessie said, thinking that she'd just have time to finish her book before she'd have to get ready to go.

She was frowning when she opened the door to Andrew a few hours later.

"What's wrong?" he asked.

"The book didn't go at all the way I'd expected," she told him. "And I didn't care for the ending one bit."

"I thought you said you'd read it before."

"I had, but I'd completely forgotten how unsatisfactory I'd found the ending. I should have realised, when I found it on the very bottom shelf of the bookshelf, that I hadn't cared for it, but some books do have to go on the bottom shelf."

"Perhaps you should write yourself a note and tuck it inside the front cover."

"I'm going to do better than that. I'm going to donate the book to a charity shop. I should have done that in the first place, but I do love the author, and the book was a gift from a dear friend. I don't want to accidentally read it again, though, so it's going this time."

Andrew nodded. "Dinner?"

Bessie locked up her cottage and then let Andrew help her climb into his hire car. On the way into Douglas, they decided where to have dinner.

"I assume Harry and Charles have arrived safely, then," Bessie said over drinks, while they were waiting for their food.

"They have, and I invited them to join us for dinner, but they both politely refused."

Bessie frowned. She'd met both men the previous month and hadn't warmed to either of them. Neither seemed interested in becoming better acquainted with the rest of the members of the cold case unit. Bessie had wondered if one or both of the men would quit before the next set of meetings, but clearly that hadn't happened.

"I hope they're both looking forward to the next case," she said after a moment.

"It's a good case for Harry, being a murder investigation," Andrew told her.

Harry Blake had been a homicide inspector with Scotland Yard before he'd retired. He was still in demand as a consultant, aside from the work that he was doing with Andrew's unit.

"I hope Charles won't be disappointed."

Charles Morris had specialised in missing persons. Also retired, he had his own team of people with whom he worked, acting as special consultants in missing person cases around the world.

"There is a missing person in the case as well. Regardless, I'm sure he's just happy to be part of the team," Andrew told her.

Bessie didn't agree. From what she'd seen, neither man was particularly interested in being part of the team, but there was no point in telling Andrew how she felt — not yet anyway. Now, though, she found herself intrigued. "A missing person?"

"We'll talk about it tomorrow," he told her, laughing as she frowned at him.

The conversation turned to books, and they had a lively debate about whether an author should ever try to continue a series that had been begun by another author. It wasn't until Bessie was crawling into bed, some hours later, that she realised that Andy had never rung her back.

CHAPTER 4

*B*essie had an appointment the next morning with Marjorie Stevens at the Manx Museum. Marjorie was the museum's librarian and archivist, and Bessie was something of an amateur historian. Over the years, Bessie had done a great deal of work on the island's wills, and recently Marjorie had given her a collection of letters to transcribe. Spanning fifty years, the letters had told the story of a young woman who'd grown up on the island and then moved to America to live with a man she'd met and married somewhat impulsively. With the last of the letters transcribed, in spite of the woman's difficult handwriting, Bessie was ready for a new challenge.

When she left the museum just before midday, Bessie found herself thinking that she should have waited to visit Marjorie until the new year. With Thanksgiving and Christmas at the Castle in the near future, and with her responsibilities to the cold case unit, Bessie wasn't certain when she'd find time to start working on the new project that Marjorie had given her.

Of course, there wasn't any rush. Marjorie was always

grateful for any work that Bessie did, regardless of how long it took her to complete it, but Marjorie also had a way of finding projects that quickly caught Bessie's interest and refused to let go until she'd completed them. That was likely going to be the case with this most recent project, Bessie realised.

Marjorie had given her a handful of diaries dating from the nineteen-twenties and thirties. They'd been written by a young woman who'd lived in Peel, and Marjorie expected them to be a fascinating account of life on the island in those years. The writer had excellent penmanship, which had initially made Bessie question why she was being given the books at all.

"Take a good look at the first page," Marjorie had suggested.

Bessie had stared at what appeared to be neatly written gibberish for a full minute before she'd looked up at her friend.

"She wrote in code," Marjorie told her. "We don't know why. Perhaps, having lived through the First World War, she'd heard about codes and felt compelled to try her own. She may explain herself in the books, of course."

"It's all in code?"

"Every page of it," Marjorie had replied brightly.

"What exactly do you expect me to do with it, then?"

"I had one of my researchers spend a few days with the first book. She managed to work out the code, which is a simple substitution code. It's possible the writer changes the code, of course, but this should get you started."

Bessie had taken the copies of the diaries and the key to the code and slid them all back into the envelope that Marjorie had given her. "I'll see what I can do," was all that she had been willing to promise.

"As ever, thank you," Marjorie had said, before giving her a hug and walking her out of the museum.

Bessie took a taxi home, and it was all that she could do not to peek at the first diary. Already, she was far too intrigued by the story, before she'd even read the first entry.

"Maybe it will all be shopping lists and recipes," she told herself as she put the envelope on the desk in her office. There was only just enough time for a light lunch before Andrew was due to collect her for the journey into Ramsey.

They were meeting at the Seaview, one of the island's most luxurious hotels, and Bessie knew that Jasper Coventry, one of the owners, would provide tea, coffee, and a generous amount of food, so she limited herself to a bowl of soup and some crackers. Andrew was at her door as she finished the washing up.

"How was your morning?" he asked when she'd let him into the cottage.

"Good, but frustrating. Marjorie has found another project that's going to take up far too much of my time."

"You'll love every minute of it," he suggested.

She sighed. "You're right, of course. I love learning about people's lives."

As they drove across the island, she told him everything she knew about the diaries she'd been given.

"The woman, Carree Quayle, had two daughters. One emigrated to New Zealand thirty years ago and when Marjorie spoke to her, she told Marjorie that she has no interest in her mother's diaries. The other daughter lived on the island until recently. She's the one who found the diaries when she was clearing out her own home before she moved to Birmingham. Apparently, she flipped through them, saw the code, and decided it was too much work to try to read them herself. She's the one who donated them to the museum. She, at least, asked for a copy of the transcripts if anyone ever transcribes them."

"What's in Birmingham?"

"Her daughter. Apparently, she's moving across to live with her and her three children. The daughter works full-time, and I gather her mother is going to look after the children in exchange for her room and board."

"I can't imagine living with any of my children," Andrew said.

Bessie shrugged. "I can't imagine living with anyone else, but I've been on my own for quite some time."

"I still miss my wife sometimes, but I have become quite accustomed to being on my own. Ah, but here we are," Andrew said as he drove into the Seaview's car park. "John's already here," he added, nodding towards John's car.

"I wonder if he's brought Doona with him," Bessie said as they walked towards the building.

Jasper greeted them in the lobby. "Good afternoon. We're delighted to have you back," he said to Andrew. "This time of year, we're delighted to have any business at all. Your friends arrived yesterday. Do remind them to let me know if they have any problems during their stay."

Andrew nodded. "Thank you. They were more than happy with their stay last month."

"But, Bessie, where's my hug?" Jasper demanded, pulling Bessie into a tight embrace. "You know you don't have to wait for one of these meetings to come and visit me," he told her as he released her. "I'm always here, working hard. You could come and have lunch with me any day. Actually, you could come and have lunch with me every day."

Bessie laughed. "I'll keep that in mind," she told him.

He walked her and Andrew down the corridor to the same conference room that they'd used during the previous meetings.

"Chef is trying out some new things. He thought your meeting would be the perfect place to test them. Do let me know what you think of everything," Jasper said as he pushed the door open.

Doona looked up from a half-empty plate of food and grinned at them. "Everything I've tried so far is delicious. I didn't get lunch, and I'm not at all sorry now."

"What was your favourite thing?" Jasper asked.

Not wanting Doona's opinion to influence her, Bessie did her best to tune out the conversation as she walked to the back of the room to consider the options. It appeared as if the chef had provided tiny samples of several main course items. She filled a plate with just about one of everything and then poured herself a cup of coffee. There were several plates of biscuits and cakes and, as Bessie took a seat next to where she knew Andrew would sit, she hoped no one would think she was being greedy if she went back for pudding later.

Hugh arrived before she'd had a chance to take her first bite. His eyes lit up when he saw the display of food and Bessie watched in awe as he filled a plate. Although she knew he was in his mid-twenties, to her he still looked not much more than fifteen, and he definitely still had the appetite of a teenager. He'd just slid into a seat when Harry and Charles arrived.

Charles had grey hair and nothing that Bessie would consider a defining characteristic. No doubt as a police inspector he'd enjoyed blending into the background everywhere he'd gone. He was frowning as he entered the room and, after he'd filled a cup with coffee, he sat down across from Bessie still looking unhappy.

Harry didn't even bother with coffee. He looked up and down the table, with his dark eyes that seemed to have seen too much, and then took a seat facing the door.

"Good afternoon, everyone," Andrew said, carrying his

own plate of food to the table. "Welcome back. We've another interesting case to consider."

"The last one didn't turn out to be all that interesting," Harry muttered.

"The last one was a success," Andrew countered. "I'm happy to report that the police in Canada were able to locate our missing person. She's alive and well and she and her mother have been speaking to one another over the past month." He paused and looked at Bessie. "Thanks to an anonymous donation, the pair will be reunited in Canada for Christmas this year," he added.

Bessie looked down at her plate, not wanting make eye contact with Doona, who she was fairly certain would be looking at her. When she'd suggested to Andrew that she fund the reunion trip, he'd insisted on splitting the cost with her. Now they were both looking forward to seeing pictures and hearing what happened when the pair finally saw one another again after so many years apart.

"Let me pass out the file for the next case, then," Andrew said. He handed each of them a large envelope.

Bessie opened hers and pulled out the file folder full of papers.

"Paul Bernhard was thirty-five when he was murdered around eighteen months ago on the third of April, in nineteen ninety-nine," Andrew began. "He was a German citizen, but he died in a flat in New York City, a place he'd never visited before. His family was unaware that he'd left Germany."

The first thing in the file was a photograph of a very handsome dark-haired man. He was laughing at something and, in the photo, he looked vibrant and happy.

"That was taken a week before his death," Andrew told them. "His fiancée shared that with the police in New York.

The next photo is from the crime scene." He looked at Bessie. "It might be upsetting," he warned her.

Bessie turned the page, and then wished she hadn't.

"How sure were they on the identification?" Harry asked dryly.

The question made perfect sense to Bessie as she stared at the photo of the badly beaten man. His face was completely unrecognisable and there was a great deal of blood, seemingly all over the room.

"They had to use DNA to make a positive identification," Andrew replied.

Bessie shuddered and turned the picture over.

"The building where the body was discovered was being renovated. It was meant to be empty, and there were security guards working there around the clock to keep people out," Andrew continued.

"So how did he get in?" Doona asked.

"That's just one of the unanswered questions from the case," Andrew replied. "You can read all of the statements from the security team who were working there the day before the body was found. According to them, there's no way the man could have been there."

"Except he was there, and his killer got in and out, presumably undetected," John said.

"You'll see in the police report that the police felt that the security was woefully inadequate," Andrew added.

"Clearly," Bessie interjected.

Andrew nodded. "I spoke to the homicide detective assigned to the case. He's Jeff Stone, and it was his opinion that most of the security was for show. They wanted everyone in the neighbourhood to think the building was secure, but, in truth, there were too many ways in and out for them to properly monitor the entire building. It didn't help that there wasn't any electricity to the building, so they didn't have any alarms in place."

Harry flipped through his pile of papers. "Are there any diagrams of the building in here? What about a floor plan for the flat where the body was actually found? How many locked doors were there between the street and the body?"

"You have a diagram of the building that shows its location on the street and identifies all of the entrances. Jeff identified seven different ways into the building. Three of them were actually being watched by security," Andrew replied.

"And the flat itself?" Harry asked.

"Was on the first floor, or, rather, what the Americans would call the second floor. Without any power, obviously the lifts weren't available, but the locations of the various stairwells are identified in the building diagrams," Andrew told him.

Bessie looked through her papers, eager to find anything that might distract her from what she'd just seen.

"The main stairwell was in the front of the building, then," John said, looking up from his file. "Presumably there was security there, though."

"There was, but there are three other staircases that were accessible from the ground floor, including one right inside the door that opened from the alley behind the building. Jeff is fairly certain that was how the victim and the killer got inside," Andrew said.

"The door was locked but not guarded?" Harry asked.

"It was locked, but with a simple deadbolt. Anyone with a decent set of lock picks could have unlocked it. You can see on the map where the guards were stationed. There were two at the front door, one on the secondary entrance on the west side, and a fourth at the secondary entrance on the south side. The door at the back was an emergency exit and would have had an alarm fitted to it if the building had had power," Andrew explained.

"So anyone could have simply let themselves in and gone exploring," Harry said with a sigh.

"In addition to the four guards at the doors, there was a fifth who did a complete circuit of the building every hour. They took it in turns, actually, rotating between guarding the doors and doing the hourly tour. Because of the size of the building and because there weren't any lifts available, a complete walk-through took about an hour, apparently," Andrew said. "That fifth guard was responsible for checking that all of the doors were shut and locked, including all of the interior doors."

"How many flats in the building?" Hugh asked.

"Hundreds, probably, but they were in the initial stages of a complete remodel. As I understand it, most of the internal doors had been removed and most of the flats had been gutted. The flat where the body was found was what they were calling their 'model apartment.' It was the only finished flat in the building, although the furniture had yet to be delivered."

Bessie glanced back at the crime scene photo. Trying to look at everything other than the body, she focussed on cream-coloured walls and what looked to be thick carpets. "Which room in the flat is this?" she asked.

"It was a one-bedroom flat, and the body was found in the bedroom," Andrew told her. "The site manager found the body at seven o'clock on the morning of the third, when he came to check that everything was ready for the furniture to be delivered. He signed in with security and then went up and unlocked the door to the flat. His statement is in your files, but, basically, he glanced into the flat, didn't notice anything amiss, and turned to leave. As he was locking the door, he remembered that there had been an issue with the carpeting in the bedroom, so he decided he'd better check that the matter had been resolved. When he opened the bedroom door, he found our victim."

"Time of death?" Harry asked.

"Between midnight and four in the morning. The carpet fitters had been there until around six the previous evening, working on the problem with the bedroom carpeting. There was some issue with the measurements that had been used, which had resulted in the piece of carpeting being slightly too small. They'd installed it anyway and tried to hide the mistake in the built-in wardrobes along the wall, but the interior designer who was in charge of decorating the model flat noticed and threw a fit," Andrew told them.

"I don't suppose our victim, Paul, was working as a carpet fitter," Charles said.

Andrew shook his head. "Everyone working on the site was thoroughly investigated. The police in New York couldn't find any link between Paul and any of them. The carpet fitters all signed in at the front desk on the second, and they all signed out around six that evening. The security guard who did the first patrol after they'd left checked the model flat to make certain it was empty. According to his statement, the workmen had left all of the doors open, but, after he'd checked the entire flat, he shut the doors to the closet and the bedroom before he locked the door to the flat."

"Were those the only doors in the flat?" Hugh asked.

Andrew checked his notes. "You've a floor plan for the actual flat. The door opened into a short corridor with what Americans call closets along both sides. About halfway down the corridor, on the left, was the loo. At the end of the corridor was a large space that the developers called the 'living area.' The kitchen was really just a nook in one corner of that area. The door to the bedroom was on the wall opposite the kitchen nook."

"And all of the closets in the corridor were shut?" Hugh asked.

"They were open when the security guard entered around half six, but he shut them all on his way out," Andrew told him. "In his statement, he's quite definite that the flat was completely empty when he went through it."

"But he would be," Harry argued. "I mean, he's not going to admit that he opened the door, glanced inside, and then shut the door again while Paul and maybe half a dozen other people were hiding inside."

Andrew nodded. "For what it's worth, Jeff is convinced that the security guard was telling the truth and that the flat was empty at half six."

"So at some point after half six and before seven the next morning, Paul and the killer found a way to get into the building and then into that flat," Harry said thoughtfully. "Did Jeff make any attempt to recreate what had happened to see if it was possible to sneak into the flat without being seen?"

"He did, and it was entirely possible. The flat was near the main stairwell, but the door couldn't be seen by anyone in the lobby. The two guards at the front door weren't even in the lobby itself, but in the entryway. Not only could they not see the entrance to the flat, but it was highly unlikely that they could have heard much from that far away," Andrew replied.

"Not even the sound of a man being beaten to death," Hugh said sadly.

CHAPTER 5

"What was the cause of death?" Harry asked.

"Trauma to the head," Andrew replied.

Bessie shuddered. "The poor man," she murmured.

Andrew glanced at her and then looked around the room. "You have the autopsy report in your file. You can read it yourselves. I'd much rather focus on what we know about Paul and why he was in New York."

"So why was he in New York?" Doona asked.

"Apparently, to meet a woman," Andrew replied.

Bessie frowned. "I thought you said he had a fiancée?"

"He did have a fiancée. He and Anja Koch had been seeing one another for over a year. He'd proposed at Christmas and they were planning for a wedding in July," Andrew told her. "He hadn't told her he was going to New York. The first she knew he was out of the country was when the police came to tell her that he'd been killed."

"Where did they live?" Harry asked.

"Berlin," Andrew replied. "Not together, obviously. Paul had a small flat in the city centre. Anja lived with her parents outside the city. They typically only saw each other on weekends, although they talked on the telephone nearly every day."

"When did he fly to New York?" Charles wanted to know.

"On the last day of March. He spoke to Anja that afternoon, telling her that he was going to be very busy with a project at work for a few days and that he'd rather she not ring him for a day or two. Apparently, that wasn't unusual. The thirty-first was a Wednesday. She told him she'd ring him on Saturday morning," Andrew said.

"Which was the day the body was found," Bessie worked out.

Andrew nodded. "Yes, although by the time she was notified, she had tried to ring him. She'd left a message on his answering machine, but had just assumed he was either sleeping late or had gone out to do some shopping. The policeman who interviewed her that evening said that when he arrived at her door, she didn't seem at all worried about Paul. In fact, her first question had been whether something had happened to her sister."

"Should we be worried about the sister?" Hugh asked.

"Maybe, but not in connection with this case," Andrew replied. "She's ten years younger than Anja, and the German detective with whom I spoke told me that she runs with a wild crowd. Regardless, she was definitely in Berlin the night that Paul died in New York."

Doona frowned. "So who was Paul meeting in New York? Why the secrecy? If there was another woman, I can see him not telling Anja about the trip, but surely he told someone where he was going?"

"You may have noticed that the only thing in the room with Paul was a battered laptop. In spite of the fact that it was badly damaged and soaked in blood, the police were able to recover some of the data from it. There they discovered a series of emails between Paul and a woman named Maria

Martone. Among other things in the emails, the pair had arranged to meet in New York City on the third of April," Andrew told them.

"So Maria killed him," Harry said. "What's so complicated about that?"

Andrew grinned. "It seems fairly straightforward, doesn't it? The problem is, the police in New York were never able to find Maria."

"There you are, Charles," Harry interrupted. "A missing person."

Charles shrugged. "Under the circumstances, I'm fairly certain Maria doesn't want to be found."

"How did Paul know Maria?" Bessie asked.

"They met in an Internet newsgroup," Andrew told her.

"I've no idea what that is," Bessie admitted.

"It's a way for people to start discussions about topics of interest, and other people all over the world can reply," Andrew told her. "You need a computer with a modem that can connect…"

"I don't think Bessie needs all of the details," Charles interrupted. "For the sake of this conversation, let's just say he met her on the Internet."

"What newsgroup?" Harry asked.

"A fan group for a role-playing game," Andrew replied. "A game called Prisoners of Cardavar. Anja was completely unaware that Paul had any interest in playing it, I should add."

"But he was interested enough to have joined a newsgroup about the subject," John said thoughtfully.

"He'd posted a few comments, asking where to find groups near him in Berlin. Maria replied to one of his comments, saying she was interested in visiting Berlin and would love a tour guide. They took the conversation to private email after that," Andrew told them. "You have copies of the subsequent emails." He glanced at Bessie and flushed. "Some of them are quite, um, descriptive of the intimacies that they were planning to share when they finally met."

"They'd never met?" Bessie asked.

"No — or, rather, they hadn't met before Paul flew to New York. Obviously, we don't know what happened in New York," Andrew replied.

"Then how could they possibly know that they wanted to become intimate?" was Bessie's next question. "One of them could have been quite unattractive or smell funny or simply not be the other's type. Surely they should have met in person before considering such things."

"They did describe themselves to one another," Andrew told her. "Although, of course, we've no evidence that Maria was honest in her description. For what it's worth, Paul was completely honest in his."

"He was a very attractive man," Doona said. "He could afford to be honest."

Andrew nodded. "He was also very clear that he was engaged and not looking for any type of commitment. It was Maria who suggested that he come over to New York for a few nights of, um, fun, before his wedding."

"So that was why he was in New York?" Hugh asked.

"Jeff Stone certainly thought so," Andrew told him. "He was convinced that Paul had gone to New York to meet Maria and that she'd killed him."

"Why would she do that?" Doona demanded.

"Maybe she wasn't really a woman called Maria," Harry suggested. "Maybe she was a man called Mark who wanted to see how it felt to kill someone. Maybe he set the whole thing up just so that he could murder a man."

Bessie frowned. "What a horrible idea."

"That's certainly one of the possibilities," Andrew said. "Jeff seems convinced that Maria is real and that she's the key to the investigation. He's spent much of the past year trying to track her down."

"What makes him so sure?" Hugh wanted to know.

"He told me it was his gut instinct, which isn't to be discounted in a trained investigator. He reached out to me because he wants someone else to go through the files and see if he's missed anything. He may be regretting the amount of time and energy he's put into hunting for Maria, seeing as he's found nothing yet."

"Paul didn't tell anyone about his trip?" Bessie asked, her mind going back over everything that Andrew had told them.

"The German police were unable to find anyone who would admit to having been told about the trip," was Andrew's very careful reply. "His parents were living in Switzerland at the time and they spoke to him only on rare occasions. His mother said that they were planning to travel to Berlin for the wedding, but that they hadn't spoken to Paul for several weeks before his death."

"What about work colleagues? What excuse did he give for missing work?" Hugh asked.

"He'd told his immediate supervisor that he was going to be working from home for the rest of the week," Andrew told them. "He worked with computers for a large manufacturing company and, apparently, he occasionally worked from home when he was working on large projects. He told his supervisor that he could get more done when he couldn't be interrupted, so he'd switch off his phone and his mobile and work. Apparently his productivity doubled when he worked from home, which pleased his supervisor."

"Why didn't he always work from home?" Doona asked. "It sounds just about perfect. You could work in your pyjamas and eat chocolate all day."

Everyone chuckled.

"Paul's supervisor reported to a manager who didn't approve of people working from home, regardless of increased productivity," Andrew explained. "I understand they'd put some sort of agreement in place that let Paul work from home a few days each month, but no more than that. The manager also didn't want everyone to start asking for the same privilege, as he doubted that most of the staff would achieve the same sort of increased productivity that Paul managed."

"He was supposed to be working from home, and he'd told his fiancée that he was working on a big project, then he flew over to New York to meet a woman he'd only ever interacted with by email," Bessie said. "Is that all correct?"

"Yes," Andrew nodded. "When the police searched his flat in Berlin, they noted that his refrigerator was empty, which suggested that he'd planned to be away, but Anja told them that his refrigerator was nearly always empty. Apparently he didn't cook, and his rubbish was full of several empty boxes and bags from various takeaways in the area that seemed to confirm that."

"Where was he staying in New York?" Bessie asked.

"He had his hotel room key in his pocket," Andrew replied. "The details are all in the file. The police found his suitcase there. It appeared as if he'd simply been living out of it, rather than having unpacked. He'd left a few toiletries in the loo, but otherwise didn't appear to have done anything to make himself feel at home."

"He had a return ticket?" John wondered.

"He did. He was due to fly back to Berlin on the fourth," Andrew confirmed.

"So he wasn't planning to stay in New York for long," Bessie said.

"Which is consistent with him going over to meet a woman," Harry suggested.

"I can't imagine meeting someone by computer," Bessie told him. "Is it something you would do?"

Harry looked surprised and then laughed. "I've been with the police for far too long to ever trust a stranger in that way. I'd demand photos first, with proof of the date, and probably more. A colleague of mine met a woman over the telephone once and that didn't end well."

"What happened?" Bessie asked.

He shrugged. "She was a dispatcher at a central location some distance from the station where he worked. They talked several times a day for weeks or even months before they finally agreed to meet. Let's just say she wasn't entirely honest about her age, her weight, or her height, and leave it at that."

Hugh laughed. "That must have been an interesting meeting."

"It was a short one, anyway," Harry told him.

"What do we know about Maria?" Charles asked.

"All of her emails are in the file, but she described herself as a twenty-five-year-old blonde with blue eyes and crooked teeth," Andrew told them. "Anja is a brunette with green eyes, and she was thirty-one when Paul died."

"So Maria was someone different," Harry said. "And Paul found that attractive."

"She also described herself as wild and carefree," Andrew told them. "In a few of her messages, she goes into some detail about some of her adventures."

"What sort of adventures?" Hugh asked.

"Nights out with large groups of friends that ended in something roughly akin to orgies back at her flat," Andrew replied flatly.

"Oh, goodness," Doona said.

"I assume she didn't give him her address," Bessie interjected.

"No, although she did talk about her neighbourhood and the views from her window. Jeff was able to work out that she had to live in one of three blocks of flats along one particular road, but he couldn't find her listed as living in any of the buildings."

"She's American?" Bessie asked as the idea occurred to her.

Andrew looked surprised and then glanced down at his notes. "I don't specifically remember her saying anything about her nationality. She lived in New York and she spoke English with American slang and spelling, so I suppose I just assumed that she was American."

"Something to look for as we read her emails," Harry suggested.

"Don't a lot of people in New York sublet their flats?" John asked. "I mean, they always seem to on television."

Andrew chuckled and then nodded. "It is fairly common, which is one of the reasons why Jeff wasn't surprised when he couldn't find Maria in any of the buildings. It's possible that she's there, but not on the lease agreement."

"And Paul didn't know anyone in New York?" Doona asked.

"Actually, two of his friends from Berlin were living there at the time. The police questioned them both, and they both denied knowing that Paul was visiting. You can read their statements in the files, but Jeff didn't see any reason to doubt them," Andrew told her.

Bessie made a note in her notebook. To her, it seemed far more likely that Paul had been murdered by someone he knew than by some stranger he'd met on his computer. If this Maria did exist, she'd probably never shown up to meet him in spite of their arrangements. If Paul had found himself unexpectedly alone in the city, it seemed reasonable to suppose that he'd ring up one of his friends from home.

"Their names?" Harry asked.

"I could keep answering questions all day," Andrew said, "or you could all go home and read the files. That seems a more productive use of my time, anyway."

Everyone chuckled and a few people nodded. Harry got to his feet.

"When do we meet again?" he asked.

"Same time and place tomorrow," Andrew replied. "I hope that will give you all enough time to read everything. Come back with questions for Jeff."

Harry nodded. "It's a thick file. It's going to be a long night." He disappeared through the door as Charles stood up.

"It is, at that," Charles said. "It's a good thing the hotel has room service. I'll see you all tomorrow."

He left the room before anyone could reply.

"As much as I'd love to suggest that we all meet for a preliminary discussion before tomorrow," Bessie said, "I think I'm going to need every spare minute between now and then to read the file."

"I hope I can find time to get through it," Doona said. "John has a late meeting and I promised the children that I'd take them out for dinner."

"And the meeting is with the Chief Constable, so I can't get out of it," John sighed. "After everything I've heard about this case, I'm really eager to get started on the file, though."

"Just do your best," Andrew told them. "I'll be here for a fortnight. I'm not expecting anyone to solve the case tomorrow."

"I thought you weren't expecting anyone to solve the case, full stop," Bessie said. At their first meeting, Andrew had insisted that they would be fortunate if they could solve a single case over the course of the year. They'd managed to find a solution to their first case, so, if Andrew had been correct, they shouldn't be able to solve any additional cases for some time.

He nodded. "All we're trying to do is find new avenues for Jeff to explore, maybe suggest other ways he might locate Maria. We've an entire fortnight to discuss it, though. Please don't worry if you can't manage to get through everything tonight."

"I'll have tomorrow morning, at least," Doona said. "John isn't as fortunate."

"Anyone want to look after the baby for me tonight?" Hugh asked. "She's always so excited to see me when I get home now that I end up playing with her for hours. Then it's bath time and story time and, well, I'll find time to read through the case, too, but I don't know that I'll have time to really think about it."

"As I said, do your best," Andrew told him. "I appreciate that you all have lives outside of this unit and that John and Hugh have full-time jobs, as well. That's why we meet only once a month and consider just a single case at a time. Please don't let this unit put any unnecessary pressure on you. I'd hate for any of you to quit."

"No worries there," John told him. "Your cases are fascinating, and I'm enjoying having a chance to work with Harry and Charles, as well."

Hugh nodded. "This is a dream assignment for a constable. If the others at the station knew about it, they'd be incredibly jealous. Does anyone mind if I take a few biscuits with me for later?"

"Take everything on the table," Andrew told him. "It's been paid for, and I believe Jasper has to dispose of anything we don't eat."

"I'll take a few things, then, too," John said. "While Doona is treating Thomas and Amy to a lovely dinner, I'll be eating in my office before my meeting with the Chief Constable."

The two men filled paper plates, but barely made a dent in the huge amount of food on the table. Andrew looked at Bessie.

"I was going to suggest going out tonight, but maybe we could just take some food home with us as well," he said.

Bessie nodded. "That will give me more time with the file," she said.

The door behind her swung open as she reached for a plate.

"I hope you're going to take that all home with you," Jasper said as he walked into the room. "I've brought you some takeaway containers from the kitchen."

By the time Andrew and Bessie had taken what they wanted and John and Hugh had done a second pass, the piles of food were considerably smaller. Jasper gave them each a large carrier bag to stack their boxes in and then he walked them through the hotel to the lobby.

"Same time tomorrow," Andrew reminded him.

"Yes, of course. I've already told Chef that he can try some of his other new ideas on you all tomorrow. Give me an idea of what worked today, though," Jasper replied.

"I tried everything, and it was all delicious," Bessie told him.

"I agree," Hugh said.

"Favourites?" Jasper asked.

"Everything," John told him. "I know that probably isn't helpful, but I truly enjoyed everything that I tried and I believe I tried everything on the table."

Jasper laughed. "I suppose it's a good problem for us to have. I'll have to work with Chef to decide which dishes can be prepared most easily and efficiently and provide a reasonable profit."

"I think I'll stick to crime," John told him.

Jasper laughed. "You're welcome to it."

As Andrew drove them back to Laxey, Bessie found herself lost in thought. While she was interested in the case and in finding Paul Bernhard's killer, she wasn't certain how she felt about being given access to the police reports. Reading about the autopsy and looking at crime scene photos didn't appeal to her in the slightest, although she was eager to read what Paul's fiancée had said in her interview.

"If you need to skip over anything in the file, you can," Andrew said as he pulled his car into the parking area next to her cottage.

"Were you reading my mind?" she demanded.

He chuckled and then patted her arm. "The others have all read autopsy reports before. Even Doona, working the front desk at the station, will have seen those and crime scene photos. They'll be new to you, and they aren't pleasant, especially in this case. I almost didn't choose this one because I wasn't certain I wanted to expose you to what's in the file."

"Why did you choose this case?"

"Because I'm pretty certain that something was missed. I feel as if Jeff focussed too much of his time on finding Maria, who may not even exist. I can't help but wonder about the security guards and about the carpet fitters. I haven't had time to read every interview yet, but I'm going to be studying what each of them said very carefully."

Bessie nodded, not yet ready to share her thoughts on Paul's German friends. After she'd read their statements, she might feel very different.

"Are you coming in?" she asked as they got out of the car.

"Maybe we could spend an hour with the file, each reading on our own, and then take a short walk before dinner," he suggested. "I'd prefer to have dinner together, if you don't mind. After that, well, let's see where we are after that."

Bessie nodded. An hour should give her enough time to

skim through the file and prioritise what she wanted to read and in what order, at the very least. After that, a walk before dinner would do her some good. As she unlocked the door to her cottage, she wondered if she would be able to find a polite way to tell Andrew to leave once they'd eaten.

CHAPTER 6

Bessie and Andrew sat side by side at the kitchen table, both with a pile of papers in front of them. The crime scene photos could wait for later, Bessie decided as she flipped past them, deliberately not letting herself look at them. Similarly, the autopsy report was set aside, along with the drawings and floor plans for where the murder had happened. She was far more interested in finding out more about the people involved, especially Paul Bernhard.

Copies of the emails had been stapled together. As Bessie picked up the packet, the date on the first page caught her eye. The message appeared to have been sent on the first of January, nineteen hundred. Of course, that wasn't possible. A quick glance through the rest of the sheets showed her that every email displayed that same date. Clearly, there had been a glitch somewhere, but Bessie didn't know enough about computers to try to guess where.

Andrew was taking notes as he read through what Bessie thought was the autopsy report. Not wanting to interrupt him, she jotted down her own note to remind herself to ask him about the dates later. The next pages in the file were copies of the various statements that had been made by witnesses, both in New York and in Germany. There wasn't anywhere near enough time for Bessie to read her way through all of them in an hour. After a moment, she decided to start with the emails.

There was a note at the top of the sheet that she read carefully.

Copies of emails that were sent between Paul Bernhard and Maria Martone. The emails have been arranged in the order in which they were sent (as best as could be determined).

A quick look through the pages showed Bessie that the copies seemed to alternate back and forth between the two senders. *Someone must have taken the time to arrange them*, she thought. That was something else to ask Andrew, actually, as she didn't really understand how email worked. The correspondence was all in English, which made sense if Maria was American.

The very first message seemed innocent enough.

To: Paul

From: MMartone

Subject: Prisoners of Cardavar Play in Berlin.

I'm planning to travel to Berlin later this year. Can you suggest where I might find a group to play with?

Paul's reply had been similarly neutral, simply recommending a few bars that allowed groups to play at tables in back rooms or quiet corners. From there, the conversation grew increasingly friendly. A few messages later, Maria described herself as a *"lonely, single girl who is always up for some fun."*

Paul's reply was something that Bessie assumed was akin to erotica, something with which she had no previous experience. Maria's reply continued along the same lines and, by the time Bessie had finished reading the emails, she felt as if she needed a shower. As she put the packet of papers down, Andrew grinned at her.

"Ready for that walk?" he asked.

"I'd much rather turn back the clock and not read what I just read," Bessie told him. "You did warn me about the emails. I should have left them to you and the others."

"They could be important," he told her. "But they are rather distasteful to read."

Bessie nodded and then got to her feet. "Let's go and get some fresh air."

They walked in silence for several minutes, past the holiday cottages and the stairs to Thie yn Traie. Feeling as if she wanted to walk until she could forget what she'd read, Bessie continued to march onwards.

"Aside from the obvious, what did you think of the emails?" Andrew asked after a while.

"Why did they all appear to have been sent on the same date, back in nineteen hundred?" she asked.

"I believe I mentioned that Paul's computer had been more or less destroyed. It was smashed and then it got covered in blood. The experts were able to recover some of the data from the hard drive, but apparently the internal clock reset to the first of January, nineteen hundred, and froze there. I was given a far more technical explanation and I may be explaining it badly, but that's more or less the reason."

"They both seemed very eager to meet, even though Paul talked about his fiancée at length."

"He didn't say very flattering things about her, though," Andrew said dryly.

Bessie nodded. In one of the earliest emails, he'd mentioned Anja, calling her a woman that he adored. As the emails progressed, he began to complain to Maria about

Anja, though. "Why do men always say that their partners don't understand them?" Bessie asked.

Andrew shrugged. "Does anyone actually understand anyone else? I think the term has become a sort of shorthand for 'I'm tired of my partner and I'm looking to cheat' more than anything else."

"That certainly seems to have been the case with Paul," Bessie said. "I don't understand why Maria was willing to go along, though."

"Some women do enjoy, er, sexual relationships without any commitment," Andrew said, seemingly choosing his words with great care.

"I'm sure they do and, if that's their choice, I'm not going to judge them for it, but there was something off about Maria's messages," Bessie said, almost to herself.

"What do you mean?"

"I've read in books that every man fantasizes about meeting a beautiful woman who simply wants to take him to bed. Maria's emails seem to be playing to that fantasy. There doesn't seem to be a real person with real feelings behind her words. I don't know, maybe it's just the way she sounded to me."

"If she truly was just looking for a bit of fun, maybe she did that deliberately," Andrew suggested. "And if she had other reasons for trying to lure Paul to New York, she had even more reason for keeping her correspondence as impersonal as possible."

"It's odd to call it impersonal when it was so graphically intimate, but it did feel artificial in some way."

Andrew nodded. "Jeff suggested that Maria might actually have been quite innocent and that she sounded odd because she didn't really have the experience to back up her words."

"According to the emails, they were supposed to meet on Thursday evening. When did Paul arrive in New York?"

"He flew to the city late on Wednesday, leaving not long after he'd spoken to Anja, actually. He checked into his hotel near midnight and apparently went straight to his room. I assume he was tired and jet-lagged and simply went to bed."

"And he was supposed to ring her mobile phone on Thursday morning to arrange a time and place to meet. Did he have a mobile with him?"

"If he did, it disappeared somewhere along the way. He had a company-issued mobile, and that was found in his flat in Berlin. As far as Anja knew, that was his only mobile."

"And he didn't ring anyone from his hotel room?"

"According to Jeff, local calls from the hotel were free and not tracked in any way. He may have rung Maria from his room, therefore."

"I assume Jeff tried to trace the number that Maria gave him in the email."

"He did. It was some sort of no-contract device, and the service had been cut off when he tried to ring it."

"Which suggests that Maria wasn't who she claimed to be or, at the very least, had a hand in what happened to Paul," Bessie suggested.

"I tend to agree, but there could be other explanations. Jeff told me that young women in the city often have a few very inexpensive no-contract phones so that they can give a number to a man and, if things don't work out, they can simply scrap the phone and not have to worry about ever hearing from the man again."

"I didn't realise such things were even available," Bessie replied.

"Apparently, they're a fairly new technology," Andrew told her.

The pair had nearly reached the new houses. Andrew stopped and took a deep breath. "I'm getting a bit tired," he told Bessie. "I think I need to turn around."

"We've walked further than I'd intended," she told him. "I'm getting quite hungry, actually."

"We've so much lovely food from this afternoon," Andrew reminded her.

They talked more about the emails as they walked back, but Bessie didn't feel as if they made any progress in the case. In spite of everything that she'd read, Bessie still felt as if Maria was a complete unknown.

As Bessie switched on the cooker to start reheating everything she and Andrew had brought back from the Seaview, she sighed. "Even if Paul believed that Maria was exactly who she claimed to be, I still can't see him flying across the Atlantic to meet her," she told Andrew. "It's a crazy idea."

"There was something in one of the emails about Paul trying to ring Maria so that they could speak in person, but they agreed that it would be too expensive."

"More expensive than flying over and staying in a hotel for several nights?" Bessie countered.

"Paul did say he needed a holiday," Andrew reminded her. "He even said he'd been planning to go to Italy for a few days, just to get away. Maria was quick to suggest that he come to New York instead."

"Presumably, Anja didn't know anything about his proposed trip to Italy, either."

"She did not," he agreed.

Bessie frowned. "I need to read all of the statements and reports and everything before we try to talk about the case. You shouldn't have to keep answering all of my questions."

"I don't mind, really, but it might be nice to talk about something else while we eat."

Bessie couldn't argue with that. When the food was hot again, the pair sat down and ate their way through everything while talking about a wide variety of subjects. By the time they were nibbling on biscuits, Bessie found herself telling Andrew about the diaries she was going to be deciphering.

"They're all in code?" he asked.

"They are, and I'm hoping that will make an interesting change from the last group of letters I transcribed. Those weren't in code, but the woman's handwriting was nearly impossible to decipher. These diaries are very neatly written, at least."

"Very neatly written code."

"Exactly."

Bessie was pouring them each more tea when a loud ringing noise made her jump.

"My mobile," Andrew said apologetically. He pulled his phone out of his pocket and frowned at it. "I need to answer this," he told Bessie, getting to his feet.

As she put the kettle back, he walked into the sitting room, talking in a low voice. Bessie had only just sat back down when he returned.

"I'm afraid I'm going to have to go," he said with a sigh. "There's something of a family emergency and I'm being dragged into the centre of it all."

"I hope nothing is wrong," Bessie exclaimed.

"One of the grandsons wants to get married, but his mother, my daughter, doesn't care for the young lady in question. I'm being asked to investigate the entire family, which, of course, I won't do." He sighed. "What I really need to do is persuade everyone to wait until I'm back in London and then arrange a meeting for me, the young lady, and her family. If they have anything to hide, they'll do their best to avoid the meeting, of course, which will confirm my daughter's suspicions."

"Do you think they have something to hide?"

He shrugged. "I think my daughter is overprotective and that no woman will ever be good enough for her darling son, but I also know that she's a good judge of character, and if there's something bothering her about the girl or her parents, well, I need to try to find out more."

Bessie let him out and then tidied the kitchen. The cottage felt oddly empty, which was ridiculous, as Bessie had always lived alone. When all of the dishes were washed and everything was back where it belonged, Bessie picked up her case file and carried it into the sitting room.

"Pretend it's just a story," she told herself in a low voice. She'd been reading murder mysteries for her entire life, after all. If she could ignore the fact that the victim had been a real person, she might be able to get through the most gruesome bits of information.

An hour later, she'd looked at all of the photos and read the autopsy report, most of which had been complicated medical jargon that she didn't understand. With all of that out of the way, she was ready to curl up with the various witness statements. By refusing to think about the fact that everything she was reading was far too real, she'd managed to get through the most difficult items. She was actually looking forward to the witness statements, hoping to actually start to learn more about the people involved in the case.

Several hours later, as Bessie found herself yawning over what one of the carpet fitters had told the police, she looked up at the clock. It was far later than she'd realised, nearly midnight. Quickly finishing the statement, which said nothing interesting, Bessie tucked a bookmark into the file and then carried it up to her office.

No one was meant to know about the cold case unit, and the police reports in the file were confidential. While Andrew hadn't specifically told her to guard the file carefully, she didn't feel right about leaving it lying around. Her desk had a locking mechanism that Bessie was certain any competent thief could unlock in seconds, but she still felt better once she'd tucked the file into a drawer and locked it.

* * *

BESSIE WAS asleep as soon as her head touched the pillow, but when she woke up at precisely six o'clock the next morning, she still felt tired. Usually she appreciated her internal alarm that never let her lie in, but today she felt more tired as she got up than she had when she'd gone to bed. Vaguely aware that she'd had unsettling dreams about horrific deaths, she showered quickly and then patted on the rose-scented dusting powder that always reminded her of Matthew.

"My life would have been completely different with you," she muttered as she let herself recall the handsome young man.

Toast, an apple, and some tea made for a quick breakfast before Bessie headed out for her walk. The curtains were all shut on Andrew's cottage as Bessie hurried past it. A strong and cold wind was blowing, and Bessie pulled her coat more tightly around herself as she reached the last cottage. Only a few paces later, she decided that the stairs to Thie yn Traie were her goal for today. When she reached them, she turned around and began a brisk walk back towards Treoghe Bwaane.

A moment later, she stopped and stared. Was it just her imagination, or was one of the windows in the last cottage not shut properly? She shook her head and looked away, staring at the sea for a moment. When she looked back at the cottage, the window still didn't look quite right. Her hand reached for her mobile phone, but she stopped herself from taking it out.

"It's just a window," she said softly. "That's less worrying than a door."

Feeling as if she'd caused far too much fuss when she'd rung Doona about the sliding door, Bessie decided to do her own investigating this time. It took her a moment to cross to the window in question. It was on the side of the house, nearer to the front of the cottage than the back, which faced the sea. Bessie found herself wondering if the window had been partially open for weeks and she'd simply not noticed.

Maggie and Thomas had removed all the curtains from this cottage, so Bessie, standing on tiptoe, was able to peer inside the window into what had been the cottage's smallest bedroom. All that she could see was a completely empty room. It seemed as if someone had pushed the window shut, but that it had stuck on one side, so that it was slightly crooked in its frame, with a small gap at the bottom in one corner.

Of course, that meant that the window was unlocked, and Bessie was certain that Maggie had told her that she'd locked every window inside every cottage before they shut up operations for the winter. Sighing, Bessie pulled out her mobile. After a moment of hesitation, she rang Maggie.

"Hello?"

"It's Bessie. There's a partially open window in the last cottage. I didn't want to ring the police again, not after they didn't find anything last time, but I thought you'd want to know."

Maggie sighed deeply. "I'll come now. If I find a body anywhere in the cottage, though, I'm going to drag it outside and then ring the police. I don't want to deal with yet another investigation inside that cottage."

The phone went silent, and Bessie slipped the device back into her pocket. *Maggie is kidding about the body*, she told herself as she began to walk away from the cottage. There was no way Maggie would actually interfere with a crime scene. As Bessie started towards home, she suddenly thought about footprints.

There were quite a few on the beach this morning, many of which Bessie assumed were still there from the previous evening when she and Andrew had strolled up and down the sand. Her own prints from her morning walk were mixed in with the others, including the ones she'd just left that led right up to the window that she had been investigating. She sighed. If someone had used that window to leave or enter the cottage, she'd probably just destroyed the evidence.

There weren't any footprints leading to any other windows or doors at any of the other cottages, she noted. For a moment she considered walking all the way around the last cottage to see if she could see any evidence of visitors, but, really, that was Maggie's concern. Maggie could do her own investigating and ring the police if she found anything worrying.

Feeling as if she wasn't up to speaking to Maggie again at the moment, Bessie walked the rest of the way home. As she walked, she wondered what was going on with that last cottage. She was vaguely aware that there were homeless people on the island. Was it possible that someone was using the cottage as temporary accommodations?

After a cup of tea and a biscuit, Bessie headed for the stairs, eager to get back to the statements she'd been reading. A loud knock on the door stopped her in her tracks.

"It will be Andrew," she told herself as she headed for the door. "Or Maggie or Doona or..." She trailed off as she reached for the handle.

CHAPTER 7

"What is going on in my cottage?" Maggie demanded as soon as Bessie opened the door. "I thought your friend Inspector Cheatham was going to keep an eye on things for us once he'd arrived. Don't tell me he's too busy with all of your top-secret meetings to pay attention to what's happening just a few cottages away from him. And I really do think, now that I've mentioned it, that you could at least tell a few of your very closest friends the truth about what's going on with the inspector and his police colleagues from London. The entire island is talking about how they came across last month and then again this month. No one seems to know why they're coming, though, although a friend of mine who works at the Seaview told me all about how your friend, Inspector Cheatham, keeps having meetings in one of the conference rooms. Apparently, the chef has been working night and day to prepare a whole range of things for the meetings."

Maggie paused for breath and Bessie seized the opportunity. "The window was partly open, then?" she asked.

For a moment, Maggie looked confused by the question,

and then she nodded. "It was partly open, which means it was unlocked, obviously. Someone had to have been in the cottage at some point in the past twenty-four hours."

"When was the last time you checked all of the windows?"

"John Rockwell and I checked them all when he was here because of the door."

"That was more than twenty-four hours ago."

"Yes, but I was down here yesterday, and I'm quite certain I would have noticed that window if it had been open."

"Were you in the last cottage?"

"You know I go in there only when I absolutely have to. No, I was in several of the others, though. I was starting to do the inspections so that Thomas and I can get an idea of what is going to need to be done before the spring."

"I can't imagine you'd have been able to see that window, then," Bessie said.

Maggie shrugged. "You didn't notice it yesterday. I'm certain you walked up and down the beach several times, didn't you?"

"I did, but I don't recall specifically looking at that cottage. I may have missed it."

"Did Inspector Cheatham walk with you? He wouldn't have missed anything out of place."

"I'll ask him about it when I next see him."

Maggie glanced behind Bessie, into the cottage. "He isn't here? I thought he'd be here."

"I don't know that he's out of bed yet, but he had a small family issue last evening. If he is up, he may be dealing with that. I haven't seen him since around half six yesterday."

Maggie frowned. "I was hoping I could speak to him. I'd feel better if he were to move to a cottage more towards the centre of the row. He isn't doing much good all the way down at this end, is he?"

"He isn't here to act as a security guard for your cottages," Bessie said sharply. "He's a paying guest, after all."

Maggie flushed. "Yes, of course, but, well, the cottage he's in needs quite a bit of work, as well. Some of the others are in better condition and might be more comfortable for him. I was thinking of him, mostly."

"I believe he'd rather be closer to me than anything else, but I'll let him know that he can move if he's interested."

"Even if he doesn't want to move this time, we may have to put him in a different cottage next month. We aren't used to renting the cottages in the winter months, and it's going to be awkward for us, having to work around him, while we're getting things ready for spring."

"I don't think he'd mind moving to the Seaview," Bessie said mildly.

"Oh, no, that's not necessary," Maggie replied quickly. "He's more than welcome and, if he truly wants that cottage, we'll find a way to work around him, as well. We're happy to have a guest off-season, really. I was hoping his friends might want to stay out here, too, actually."

"I believe they're both happier at the Seaview. It's a lovely hotel, of course, with maid service and room service and all of the most modern amenities."

Maggie frowned. "We are considering putting a restaurant in the last cottage, but we won't be doing that until later in the year."

"The food at the Seaview is excellent, as well. No doubt Andrew's friends are happy there."

Maggie leaned forward and lowered her voice to a whisper. "But what are they doing here?" she asked.

Bessie shook her head. "You should ask Andrew that," she suggested, hoping to dodge the question.

"I did ask him, and Dan Ross has asked him a dozen or more times."

Dan Ross was one of the most annoying people that Bessie knew. A reporter for the local newspaper, he spent nearly all of his time harassing people, trying to get them to tell him things that would get him an interesting headline. His ultimate aim was to break a big enough story that he would get offered a job with one of the big national newspapers in the UK. As much as Bessie disliked him, she continued to hope that his dream would come true one day soon. Anything that got him off the island had to be a good thing, she reasoned.

"Maybe you should ask the men themselves," Bessie suggested, knowing that neither Harry nor Charles would tell Maggie or Dan anything.

Maggie made a face. "I was at the Seaview last month while they were here. They were having dinner in the restaurant, at separate tables, I might add. They certainly didn't look as if they were friends with one another, even if they're both friends with Inspector Cheatham. One of them looked nice enough, but he was on his mobile the entire time, talking quietly to what seemed to be an entire group of people. The other man was scary-looking, and I didn't dare try to speak to him."

Bessie hid a smile. Maggie's descriptions of Charles and Harry were spot on. Harry probably was quite scary-looking if you didn't know him. Bessie wasn't afraid of him, exactly, but she was rather intimidated by him. And Charles did seem to spend a lot of time on his mobile, talking to the team he worked with back in London. He'd been involved in a missing person case the last time he'd been on the island, and he'd spent much of his spare time working on that case, rather than the one the cold case unit was considering. In the end, the missing man had turned up unharmed and only slightly embarrassed that he'd caused such an uproar.

"Was anything disturbed in the cottage?" Bessie asked, trying to change the subject more than anything else.

"Not that I could tell. Thomas and I were considering switching the alarm back on, but it was nothing but trouble last time. I really don't know what to do."

They'd had an alarm system installed in the last cottage, but when they'd tried to use it, it seemed to be easily triggered by the strong winds that blew across the beach. After the police had been to check the cottage several times in just a few days, they'd turned the system off and decided not to have alarms put into the rest of the cottages.

"I'll talk to Andrew when I see him. Maybe he'll have some ideas," Bessie offered.

"I'd really appreciate that," Maggie said quickly. "And now I must go. I left Thomas having breakfast. No doubt he's finished now and will be trying to load the dishwasher. He'll be mixing up what goes where and putting the plates in all wrong, I'm certain."

Bessie watched as Maggie walked back down the beach towards the car park that was near the centre of the row of the cottages. The curtains were still drawn on Andrew's cottage, so Bessie shut the door and then went and got her case file. For the next few hours she read statements and took careful notes. By midday, she was exhausted from paying such close attention to everything that she was reading, and she was starving.

There were just a few things left from yesterday's meeting, so she reheated them and then made herself some more toast to go with them. Lunch out of the way, she found herself feeling restless. Another walk on the beach would help clear her head, and maybe Andrew would spot her and join her. She'd prefer to discuss the issues with the last cottage with him before their unit meeting, if possible.

A brisk stroll to Thie yn Traie and back did help clear

Bessie's head. It also gave her a chance to notice that Andrew's car was missing from the parking area near her cottage. The man had obviously gone out somewhere, and Bessie could only hope that he wouldn't forget to collect her before the meeting at the Seaview.

Back in her cottage, she read through her notes and the questions she'd jotted down from what she'd read. Feeling as if she ought to go through it all again, Bessie felt reluctant to reopen the file. Clearly, her brain needed a break, and she knew just the thing to clear her head.

Half an hour later, she'd painstakingly worked out the first page of the first diary entry. As she'd been working letter by letter, carefully using the key she'd been given, Bessie hadn't paid any attention to the words she'd deciphered. Now she sat back and read the first entry out loud.

"'Today is the first day of January, in the year nineteen twenty. I'm Carree Kewish and I'm twenty years old. I'm also in love, which is why I'm writing this in code. My sister, Breeshey, is only fifteen and she's far too nosy for her own good.

The man I intend to marry is one Harold Hartner. He only recently moved to the island from Liverpool to work as an apprentice to the local blacksmith. He's very strong and very handsome, and I'm looking forward to being Mrs. Carree Hartner one day.'

The rest of the page had been taken up with the words Carree Hartner written over and over again. Bessie frowned when she realised that she hadn't even noticed the repetition. *I really should pay more attention to what I'm doing*, she thought as she put the copy of the diary and her transcription into a drawer. Clearly, Paul Bernhard was on her mind more than she'd realised.

Andrew knocked on the door a few minutes before two. "I'm late," he said apologetically. "It's been a long day, and I've not had much chance to study the case, either."

"I hope things are better at home," Bessie said as she

grabbed her handbag and followed Andrew to the car. She'd been just about to ring for a taxi when he'd arrived, but he didn't need to know that.

"Things are improving, but still tense," he told with a sigh. "Everything is going to have to wait now until I'm back in London. As if that weren't enough, the island's Chief Constable rang this morning and asked me for a meeting."

"What did he want?"

"Officially, to assure me that he and the entire Isle of Man Constabulary support what we're doing. Unofficially, he wanted to know about the case. I gave him as little information as I could, but I won't be surprised if he asks for more details."

"I don't understand why he's getting involved. Surely he has enough to do already."

"Within police circles, the unit got a lot of notice last month when we solved that case. I think he's hoping to grab some of the credit if we manage to solve another one."

Bessie sighed. "I thought the unit was a big secret."

"I would prefer it if the wider world didn't know anything about the unit, but it needs to be discussed within the policing community. That's how we're going to hear about other cases that we might want to consider," he explained.

"I see," Bessie said, wondering if the policing community actually knew about her personally, or if they simply knew that Andrew had formed a unit from among his acquaintances. It was odd to think that people she'd never met might be discussing her and her role in the unit.

"I hope you found time to read through the file," Andrew said a moment later.

"I did, and I've a long list of questions," Bessie told him.

"Excellent," he replied. "I hope you found time, either last night or this morning, to enjoy a book or a long walk on the beach, as well. I truly don't want these cases to take over your life."

"I decoded the first page of those diaries that Marjorie gave me."

"And did you learn anything interesting?"

Bessie laughed. "I learned that at twenty, Carree believed that she was going to marry an apprentice blacksmith named Harold Hartner."

"But she doesn't?"

"I'm not certain, but I doubt it. She was Carree Quayle when she died, but I suppose she could have been married more than once. I rather suspect that Harold is going to be nothing but a passing fancy, but I could be mistaken."

"You will let me know, won't you?"

"Of course," Bessie replied, wondering if he was actually interested or simply being polite. "When I walked past the last cottage, one of the windows was partially open," she added.

Andrew muttered something that might have been a curse. "Which window?" he asked.

"One of the ones on the side facing away from the other cottages. It was the one furthest from the beach, and it was just slightly ajar, mostly on one side," she explained.

"What did John say?"

"I didn't ring John," Bessie told him. "There seemed little point in bothering the police again. Last time it turned out to be nothing, after all."

"You should have rung John," Andrew said, glancing at Bessie. "It sounds very much as if someone is routinely breaking into that cottage, which is a very serious matter."

"I rang Maggie. She came down and went through the cottage. Nothing had been disturbed."

"And now Maggie has trampled through any evidence of a break-in that may have been there."

Bessie sighed. "It's cold and windy at the moment. If someone is breaking into the cottage to get out of the weather, well, I'm not certain I want him or her caught. The cottage is empty. Whoever it is isn't doing any harm."

"If someone is breaking into that cottage, it will be because he or she doesn't have a safe place to stay. I'd much rather find and help the person than turn a blind eye," Andrew countered.

"Maggie was wondering if you had any ideas for ways to secure the cottage," Bessie replied after a pause. "She thought maybe you could move into one of the cottages closer to the centre of the row."

Andrew shook his head. "I'm quite happy where I am, next to your cottage. The last thing I want to do is pack my things and move."

"She was talking about trying to use the security system again. The last time they used it, the alarm kept going off every time it was windy."

"So, every night?" Andrew asked.

Bessie laughed. "Sadly, I think you may be right."

Andrew turned into the car park for the Seaview and found a space near the door. "We're only a few minutes late," he said. "Let's worry about Maggie and her problems on the way home. For now, we need to focus on Paul Bernhard."

As Bessie got out of the car, she heard a voice calling her name.

"Bessie? My goodness, what a surprise," the voice said.

Frowning, Bessie turned around and glared at the man who was walking towards her. "Dan Ross," she said tightly. "What brings you here?"

The man shrugged. "I was in the area, following up on a story, and I thought I'd come here for lunch."

Bessie glanced at her watch. "It's a bit late for lunch."

"I'm a busy man. I eat when I can," Dan replied. "Ah,

Inspector Cheatham, I'd heard you were back on the island, but I wasn't certain the rumour was true."

"Good afternoon," Andrew said. "I hope you'll excuse us, but we're late for a meeting." He took Bessie's arm and began to lead her away.

"A meeting, is it?" Dan called after him. "That would be why your friends, Harry Blake and Charles Morris, are on the island again, then? I can certainly understand why three police inspectors would be having a meeting. Inviting John Rockwell along makes perfect sense, as well. What I don't get is why Bessie is here. She and Doona, and even Hugh, seem odd choices for a meeting between police inspectors, wouldn't you say?"

"Perhaps the meeting is nothing to do with our having been police inspectors," Andrew replied, still walking across the car park with Bessie as he spoke. "Maybe we all share the same fascination with some obscure American playwright or French Impressionist painters or with Catherine the Great."

Dan stared at him. "You're suggesting your monthly meetings are some sort of fan club for a former Russian empress?"

"Anything is possible," Andrew said brightly before he led Bessie into the hotel. Dan followed, but he was intercepted by Jasper before he could speak again.

"Mr. Ross, I'll simply remind you that you are not welcome here if you're going to be interrogating our guests. You are also not welcome to sneak around and try to over-hear things that are not your concern," Jasper told the reporter. "Why are you here?"

Dan flushed. "I came to have lunch," he said tightly. "But as it appears I'm not welcome, I'll take my business elsewhere."

"You're more than welcome to have lunch," Jasper countered. "As long as you stay at your table and leave our other guests to enjoy their meals."

Dan looked as if he wanted to argue, but after a moment he shrugged. "The food here is generally excellent."

"Will you be writing a review of today's meal?" Jasper asked.

"Of course not," Dan snapped. "I'm an investigative journalist, not a food critic."

Jasper nodded. "Let me have someone show you to the dining room," he offered.

He walked over and spoke to the young man behind the desk. After a moment, the man picked up the phone and pressed a button. Only seconds later, a young woman rushed out from the office behind the desk. Bessie was happy to see Sandra, who had previously worked at the shop near Bessie's cottage.

"Ah, Sandra, please escort Mr. Ross to the dining room," Jasper said. "We wouldn't want him getting lost along the way."

Dan scowled as the woman nodded and then smiled at him. "Right this way, sir," she said smartly.

Bessie said a quick "hello" to Sandra before the woman escorted Dan out of the foyer.

Andrew waited until the pair had disappeared down the corridor before he spoke.

"Thank you. I'd rather he not know exactly where we have our meetings. I understand technology is making rapid advances in the area of miniature listening devices."

"I believe we'll move your next meeting to a different room," Jasper said. "And perhaps you should meet in a different room every time you meet here. We have ten conference rooms, after all."

Andrew grinned at him. "It might be wise to move us

around occasionally. Anything that frustrates Dan Ross is a good thing."

Jasper laughed. "I'm sure he's sitting in the restaurant feeling frustrated right now."

He escorted Andrew and Bessie to the conference room door. Andrew knocked and then opened the door.

Everyone else was already there, sitting around the table. Hugh, Doona, and John had plates of food and drinks in front of them. Charles also had a drink, but nothing to eat. Harry simply had his case file on the table in front of him.

"I'm sorry we're late," Andrew said. "Bessie and I will just get what we need and we'll get started."

CHAPTER 8

*B*essie poured herself a cup of coffee and put a few biscuits onto a plate. Nothing else was particularly tempting to her today.

"I didn't get lunch," Andrew explained as he filled a plate with a little bit of everything. He got himself coffee, and then he and Bessie joined the others at the table.

"I'm starving, so I'm going to eat for a few minutes," Andrew said. "While I'm doing that, what did you all think of the case? Any obvious suspects or things that you're certain Jeff missed?"

"The most obvious suspect is Maria," Harry said. "Find her and the case will be solved."

"I have some ideas of where Jeff can look for her," Charles said. "I have a friend who knows New York well. I know Jeff narrowed down his search to three buildings, but I believe my friend could get that down even further. For someone who was clearly hiding her identity, she wrote a lot about what she could see from her window."

Harry nodded. "I'd be willing to bet that the view she described wasn't really hers," he countered.

"I think you're overthinking this," Charles replied. "If she didn't want him to know where she lived, why bother describing her view at all?"

"Because she didn't want him to know where she lived," Harry replied. "She was able to make it seem as if she were telling him all about herself, while actually giving him completely false information."

"In the earliest emails, when she first talks about her flat, they haven't even discussed meeting yet, or, rather, she's talked about wanting to visit Berlin, rather than him coming to New York. She had no reason to lie at that stage," Charles insisted.

Harry shrugged. "Feel free to pursue that line of inquiry. For what it's worth, I don't think you'll ever find a woman named Maria Martone anywhere in New York, and if you do, she won't be the one who was writing to Paul."

"So who do you think he was corresponding with?" Charles asked.

"Someone pretending to be exactly what he was looking for," Harry replied. "A man, maybe, or more likely, a group of men who do this sort of thing regularly."

"There are groups of men who do this regularly?" Doona asked.

Harry shrugged. "Perhaps not many, not yet, but as the Internet grows and people use it more and more to make connections, it's inevitable that people will start to use it for criminal means."

"So you think some gang of men reached out to Paul on this gaming newsgroup specifically to murder him?" Charles asked.

"I suspect they were after money, rather than looking to murder him, but maybe they weren't expecting him to come to New York. Maybe he took them by surprise and, when they couldn't produce Maria, maybe he threatened to ring the police or maybe he started a fight. There are any number of possibilities."

"How could they get money from him?" Bessie asked, feeling confused.

"Maria started out talking about visiting Berlin," Harry reminded her. "What if she started to plan the trip and then told Paul that she didn't have quite enough money for her plane ticket? I'm sure he would have been happy to send her a few hundred dollars' worth of Deutsche Marks or euros, whichever they were using at the time."

"And she could have been emailing back and forth with dozens or even hundreds of men," Andrew added. "Except she may well have been a man or, as Harry said, a group of men."

Bessie sighed. "As I said before, I can't imagine agreeing to meet in person some random stranger that I'd only ever spoken to over the Internet. It seems far too risky to me."

"You simply have to arrange to meet them in a public place," Doona told her. "There are a lot of matchmaking agencies popping up, and that's what they suggest, anyway."

"Matchmaking agencies?" Bessie repeated.

Doona nodded. "I was considering trying one a while back, but they had just a handful of customers on the island and I didn't want to have to go across just to have dinner with a stranger that I'd been matched with via computer."

"And now you aren't interested in finding someone," John suggested.

Doona laughed. "I'm not interested in finding anyone else," she told him.

"So, if Maria wasn't actually Maria and she didn't actually live where she pretended to live, how do you propose to find her?" Charles asked Harry.

"I've already joined the newsgroup. I'm just sitting back and waiting for Maria to find me," he replied.

"You've done what?" Charles demanded.

"I've joined the newsgroup and a few other, similar ones. I reckon within a few days I'll be a target for the same person or people that targeted Paul on at least one of the newsgroups."

"That's an interesting idea," John said.

"Indeed," Andrew said. "What's happened thus far?"

"I've been working hard on learning enough about the three different games I'm pretending that I play so that I can blend into the crowd. Later today, I plan to ask if anyone can suggest any new venues in London for gameplay. I'm hoping that will invite Maria, whatever she's calling herself now, to reach out in the same way she did with Paul," Harry replied.

"Keep me informed," Andrew told him.

"Oh, I will. I'll email you copies of everything that I receive and my replies," Harry promised.

"John, thoughts?" Andrew asked.

"I had quite a few of them, and now I'm second-guessing myself, based on everything I've heard since I've been here," he said with a rueful grin. "Charles and Harry are both focussing on Maria, whether that's who she truly was or not. I'm more concerned about the men that we know were there when Paul died."

"Meaning?" Harry asked.

"Meaning the men who were working on the building site where the body was found, mostly. Paul didn't know New York, and from what I can tell, his hotel wasn't anywhere near the building where the body was found. It seems highly unlikely that he stumbled into that building accidentally, so someone must have arranged a meeting either there or nearby," John explained.

Andrew nodded. "I don't think Jeff spent enough time looking into the background of the various employees on the site. It's possible that one of them had some tie to Paul that Jeff failed to find."

"There were dozens of people working on the site," Hugh said. "That's a lot of backgrounds to investigate."

"He didn't ask any of them about the game that the newsgroup was about," Andrew said. "I think that was a mistake."

"I agree. It's a tenuous link, but there could be something there," John said.

"Why didn't Anja know that he played?" Doona asked. "I find that odd."

"Maybe he didn't play when she was around," Hugh suggested. "She lived with her parents and stayed with him only occasionally. Presumably, that left him with quite a bit of time on his hands to play games."

"Has anyone here ever played Prisoners of Cardavar or anything similar?" Andrew asked.

Bessie glanced around the table. After a moment, Hugh flushed and nodded.

"I played Prisoners of Cardavar a bit when I was younger. It was kind of popular for a few years when I was a teenager, but it was really complicated. Games could go on for days or even weeks. I got fed up with it and quit before I even fully understood the rules," he told them.

Andrew nodded. "You seemed reluctant to admit to that," he said mildly.

Hugh shrugged. "The kids who played weren't exactly the popular kids. I mean, I wasn't either, but, well, it wasn't the sort of thing that anyone talked about at school. Some of the other kids would have made fun of me if they'd known."

"Which may explain why Paul didn't tell Anja that he played," John suggested.

"They were getting married. Was he going to quit playing once that happened?" Doona wondered.

"He doesn't sound as if he's considering giving up in his

posts on the gaming newsgroup," John said. "He talks about looking for new places to go to play."

"But after the first few emails, he and Maria don't talk about the game at all," Bessie pointed out.

"They were rather busy discussing other things," Doona said dryly.

Everyone chuckled.

"I find it hard to believe that Maria was much of a gamer," Hugh said. "From what she told Paul, I can't imagine when she found time to play that sort of role-playing game. As I said before, games could go on for days and, from what she told Paul, she was having wild sex nearly every night."

"More proof that she simply doesn't exist," Harry said.

"Maybe she was simply trying to be what she thought Paul wanted," Charles interjected. "Maybe she was, well, not the most attractive woman in the world. Maybe she thought that Paul would be more interested in her if he thought she was, um, free with her favours, shall we say?"

"Or maybe she was trying to lure him in so that she could scam him out of a fortune," Harry suggested.

"Bessie, what do you think?" Andrew asked.

"I'm still struggling to believe that Paul went to New York to meet Maria, whether she was who she claimed to be or not. I want to know more about the two men he knew in the city," she replied.

"They were both interviewed by the police," Charles said. "Neither of them had spoken to Paul in months and neither knew he was in the city."

"Assuming they were telling the truth," Bessie murmured.

Charles raised an eyebrow and then gave her a small nod. "Yes, of course," he said, slightly condescendingly.

"I didn't spend much time on their statements," Andrew said. "Let's talk about them for a minute."

He checked his notes, and then opened his folder and

turned to a page near the back. "Their names are Max Wolfe and Leon Weber," he said. "Max is thirty-six and single. He'd been in New York for around six months when Paul died."

"He was there on a two-year secondment from his job in Berlin. He worked in banking," Bessie told him when he fell silent. "He may still be there, of course. The secondment should have finished in October, if it truly was for two years."

"I can have Jeff check to see where Max is now," Andrew said, making a note.

"In his interview, he seemed surprised to hear that Paul had travelled to New York and hadn't rung him," Doona said. "From what he said, they'd been friends for over ten years."

"He also said that they'd talked about Paul coming to see him," Bessie added. "He said something about suggesting that Paul have a weekend in New York before he got married and tied down."

"He's a link to Prisoners of Cardavar, too," Hugh said. "Max said he hadn't known that Paul played, but that it was something he himself had played on a handful of occasions."

"But he denied even knowing that there was an Internet newsgroup for the game," Doona interjected.

Bessie sighed. "I want a chance to speak to him and to Leon Weber myself," she said. "If I were travelling to a strange city to meet a stranger, I'd make sure my friends in the city knew I was there."

"Do you think they were both lying?" Andrew asked.

"I don't know. It's impossible to tell from their statements, not when I haven't ever met them," Bessie replied with a sigh.

"It sounded as if Paul was closer to Leon than to Max. Leon did introduce Paul to his fiancée, after all," Doona said.

"I missed that," Hugh said.

"According to Leon's statement, he and Anja went out a few times, but it wasn't anything serious. Then Leon met someone else and ended things with Anja," Bessie told him. "He claims that he felt bad about breaking things off, so he introduced Anja to Paul, who had also just come out of a relationship."

"And they fell madly in love," Doona added. "Although Leon sounded quite surprised about that. He said he thought that they'd have some fun together, but he never expected them to get engaged."

"How did Leon end up in New York?" Hugh asked, flipping through his file as he spoke.

"The woman that he left Anja for was American," Bessie explained. "She was working in Berlin for three months, and when she left to go back to New York, Leon decided to go along."

"Wouldn't he need some sort of visa or work permit or something?" Hugh asked.

"His mother is American, although she and her family moved to Germany when she was sixteen. She'd spent long enough in the US to be able to pass along US citizenship to her son, though," Bessie replied.

"Were Leon and his American girlfriend still together when Paul died?" Hugh asked.

Bessie shook her head. "According to Leon's interview, the relationship didn't last long once they'd arrived in New York, but he was enjoying life in America and wasn't in any hurry to go back to Berlin."

"How long had he been in New York before Paul died?" Andrew asked. When Bessie looked over at him, he shrugged. "I've read the entire file, but I've forgotten some of the details."

"He'd moved to New York in early December, so around four months before Paul died," Bessie told him. "I really want to know if he's still there."

Andrew made a note. "I'll have Jeff try to locate both men," he told her.

"I think he should interview them both again," Bessie replied. "Although I don't suppose either of them is going to change his story after all this time."

"What did Leon say about Prisoners of Cardavar?" Hugh asked.

"He claimed to know next to nothing about the game and that he had no idea that Paul was interested in that sort of gaming," Bessie answered.

"Leon and Max must know one another," Hugh said. "Leon didn't know that Max played, either?"

"Actually, apparently the two men had never met. Max and Paul had been friends for years, having met at one of Paul's first jobs after he'd finished university. He'd met Leon only a few years before his death," Bessie told him. "Again, they'd met at work. Leon told the police that when he'd told Paul he was moving to New York, Paul had mentioned that one of his other friends had moved there recently. Leon said that Paul suggested that he should go over and visit them both, as he thought they'd get along, but that nothing ever came of it."

"What did Max say about Leon?" Hugh asked.

"Something similar. Apparently, he spoke to Paul occasionally and he remembered Paul mentioning that another of his friends was moving to the city, but he couldn't recall the man's name or anything else about him," Bessie reported.

"If you were moving to a strange city, wouldn't you want to make as many connections as possible, even if they were fairly tenuous ones?" Doona wondered.

"Leon was moving to be with his girlfriend, though," Hugh pointed out. "No doubt she had her own social circle in the city."

Everyone fell silent for a moment. Bessie finished her

drink and thought about getting more. It felt as if the meeting was winding down, though.

"Let's see if we can wrap this up," Andrew said. "Charles, you're going to see if your friend in New York can help find the building where Maria claimed she lived."

"If he can, I'll suggest that he go door to door through the building to see if anyone can remember a woman named Maria who may have lived there eighteen months ago," Charles said. "He's good at getting people to talk to him, and buildings that large always have a few nosy neighbours who keep track of everyone else. If Maria really did live there, he'll find her."

"Except she didn't live there, because she doesn't exist," Harry said. "I'm going to keep poking around the newsgroups. I'll spend some time on the Prisoners of Cardavar group, but I think I'll spend more time on some of the others. If I'd murdered someone I'd met through a newsgroup, I think I'd move on to a different group pretty quickly."

"Maybe one that has nothing to do with role-playing games," Hugh suggested.

Harry shrugged. "Except I'm going to guess that our killer either plays or spent some time learning enough about the games to be able to talk about them with authority. He or she may not want to take the time to learn about some other hobby. Having said that, I may drop into a few other groups, maybe some of the more active of the ones in other niche hobby areas, and make a comment or two. You never know."

Andrew nodded. "I'm going to talk to Jeff about speaking again to the security guards and the men who were working on the model flat," he told John. "He needs to talk to them about Prisoners of Cardavar, if nothing else."

"He should also ask them if they know either Max or Leon," John suggested. "I assume there wasn't anything that linked either man to the site where the body was found."

"I don't believe so, but I'll double-check with Jeff. Does anyone remember reading anything in the file about any link?" Andrew asked, looking around the table.

"I don't recall either man being specifically asked about the location where the body was found," Bessie said thoughtfully. "They were asked for alibis on the night of the murder, and neither had one, but they both claimed to have been far away from the site. Did Jeff investigate the companies where they worked for any links?"

Andrew made another note. "He may well have and that information simply never made it into the file," he told Bessie. "Sometimes, things that don't seem to go anywhere don't end up being officially noted."

She nodded.

"And the last thing we want from him is information on the current whereabouts of Max and Leon," Andrew added. "Max should be back in Berlin, assuming his assignment wasn't extended. I'm tempted to fly over and speak with him myself."

"I want to come along," Bessie said quickly.

Andrew patted her hand. "If I go, I'll take you along," he promised. "You'd probably have better luck getting information out of him than I would, anyway. Everyone seems to talk to you."

Bessie flushed. "I've never been to Berlin," she said, wanting to change the subject.

"If that's all, I'm going to go and see what else I can learn about Prisoners of Cardavar," Harry said. "If I do get any replies to my posts, I need to be ready to talk about the game."

He was on his feet and out the door before anyone replied. Charles was right behind him, muttering "later" under his breath as he left.

"We aren't meeting again until the day after tomorrow, correct?" Bessie asked Andrew.

"Yes, that's right," he confirmed.

"Dinner at my cottage tomorrow night, then?" Bessie asked the others.

"Yes, please," Hugh said quickly. "I'll even bring pudding."

"In that case, I'll be there," Doona laughed.

"I'll bring Doona," John offered. "And we'll bring both dinner and pudding as well. I'll be coming from Ramsey, so I'll get something at the bakery there."

"Maybe I'll be able to bring a few answers to some of our questions," Andrew said with a grin.

CHAPTER 9

*T*he meeting had left Bessie feeling restless. "I want to do some window shopping in Ramsey," she told Andrew as they walked to his car. "If you can leave me there, I'll get a taxi home again."

"I can, if you'd prefer to be alone. Otherwise, I'm more than happy to join you for some shopping. I spent far too much time indoors this morning. A walk through Ramsey town centre might clear my head," he replied.

Although Bessie was quite used to doing things on her own, she didn't mind company, or at least that's what she told herself as she smiled at Andrew. "You're more than welcome to join me," she said, feeling as if she was exaggerating only slightly.

"If we take our time, maybe we can get dinner somewhere nice before we head back to Laxey," Andrew suggested.

Feeling slightly better about the idea, Bessie nodded and then got into Andrew's car. He drove into the town centre and parked in the car park near the large bookshop that was one of Bessie's favourite places in the world.

"Should we save the bookshop for last?" he asked as they got out of the car.

Bessie didn't usually have enough self-discipline to save the bookshop for last. "I suppose," she said reluctantly as Andrew offered his arm.

He laughed. "From your tone, I get the impression you'd rather look at books first."

"I'm just afraid we might run out of time if we do our other shopping first."

"And we'd both much rather spend our time looking at books than anything else, anyway," he added. "Let's start here, and if don't get anywhere else, well, no harm, really."

Bessie laughed. "I couldn't agree more."

Inside the large shop, Bessie hesitated. *Where do I want to start today?*

"I'm going to take a look around the gift shop section first," Andrew told her. "I need to take a few things home for my children and the neighbour who is keeping an eye on my flat for me."

Bessie nodded, not really listening. A large display of bargain books had caught her attention. The sign over the display said "Curl up With a Cosy Mystery Today," an invitation that she was all too eager to accept. Andrew found her an hour later, in the mystery section of the shop, studying the back of a thick hardcover.

"What have you found, then?" he asked.

"I've put half a dozen books behind the counter," she told him. "That way, I don't have to carry them all around with me as I shop. I was just wondering about this one, but I don't think I will buy it after all."

He raised an eyebrow and held out his hand. She passed him the book and watched as he read the back cover.

"I thought you preferred cosy mysteries. This is anything but cosy," he remarked as he put the book back on the shelf.

"In light of the things I read about this case, I thought maybe I would enjoy something different, but I don't believe that's the book for me, regardless."

"I can recommend a few authors if you want to try some police procedurals. I'm very particular about the ones I read, because so many of them get things wrong."

Bessie thought about it for a moment and then shook her head. "I think I'll stick to the familiar for now. As I said, I've chosen half a dozen books already, and I believe they have a few more for me that they were getting ready to post."

An arrangement with the shop had them sending Bessie boxes of books at least once a month, based on her list of favourite authors. It saved Bessie having to carry bags of books around the town when she did come into Ramsey, and it meant that she never missed a new release.

"I've been lost in the gift department for the last hour," Andrew said. "Would you mind spending another half an hour or so here while I look at books?"

Bessie laughed. "Of course not. If I run out of books to look at, I'll just sit down in a quiet corner with one of the books I'm planning to purchase and read until you're ready to go."

He found her again, forty-five minutes later, in the biography section of the shop.

"I'm finished, but I don't want to rush you," he told her as she slid a book back onto the shelf.

"I'm ready to go," she told him. "I rarely spend this much time here when I'm on my own, as I always feel as if I must rush to get things done. This was a lovely luxury, actually."

"I'm pleased to hear that."

"Anne Boleyn seems to be very popular at the moment," she remarked as they crossed to the counter. "There were several new biographies of her."

"Everyone is suddenly interested in her," the girl behind

the till replied. "Her and Mary, Queen of Scots. I believe there's been something on the telly about them, but I don't really watch telly."

"Me either," Bessie said. "It's good to hear that the telly is encouraging more people to read, though, I suppose."

The girl laughed. "I suppose you're right about that." She brought out the box of books that they'd been filling for Bessie, and Bessie bought those along with the ones she'd selected for herself. The total made her blush, as it seemed an indulgence, even though it was one she could easily afford. She felt slightly better when Andrew's total, just from the gift shop, was more than hers, and once the shop assistant had added in the two books he'd selected, Bessie felt a good deal less guilty.

They carried their purchases back to the car and then had a slow meander along the row of shops, starting on one side of the street and then crossing over to the other on their way back. Andrew bought a few things in the large toyshop for the youngest grandchildren in his family, and Bessie found another book she wanted in one of the charity shops. In spite of the food that she'd enjoyed during the meeting, Bessie found herself getting quite hungry as they returned to Andrew's car.

"Dinner?" he asked as he added the rest of their purchases to the boot. "Because I'm far hungrier than I ought to be."

"Yes, please," Bessie quickly agreed.

"Is there a nice pub nearby?" he asked. "Ideally, somewhere that does cottage pie."

"Right across the road."

Andrew smiled. "Perfect."

The pub was nearly empty when they walked in a few minutes later.

"Sit anywhere," the bartender called. "Order from me if you want food."

An hour later, Bessie was feeling quite content as Andrew drove them back to Laxey. Dinner had been very good and she had a large pile of new books to read. There was nothing further to do on the case until Andrew had heard back from Jeff, which meant she could read without feeling guilty, especially since she'd already decoded the first diary page and found nothing at all interesting there.

Back at Treoghe Bwaane, Andrew insisted on carrying Bessie's bags inside for her.

"And now, I imagine you'd quite like to curl up with your new books and forget about the real world for a few hours," he suggested.

"I would, rather," Bessie agreed. *Sometimes honesty was better than being polite,* she thought.

He laughed. "I need to go and send a long email to Jeff and then type up all of my notes from the meeting. Once I've done those things, I'll probably settle in with one of my new books. I'll see you in the morning."

Bessie walked him to the door and then watched as he walked back to his car to gather up his bags. As he headed for his cottage, she pushed her door shut and sighed. While she enjoyed spending time with Andrew, she enjoyed being alone at least as much.

Selecting which book to read first was a delightful dilemma for Bessie. After a moment's hesitation, she selected the latest book in a long series, one that she'd enjoyed since the very beginning. With a cup of tea and a handful of biscuits on the table next to her, she sat down in her favourite chair and opened the book.

Half an hour later, the tea and the biscuits were gone. Bessie slid a bookmark into the book and sat back with a sigh. Maybe it was the book or maybe it was her, but she simply couldn't get lost in the story. Having read the first dozen or more books in the series, she felt as if she knew many of the characters, but for some reason they all seemed off. As she put the book on the table, she reread the cover.

Unlike the previous books in the series, this one credited a coauthor. While she'd noticed that before she'd purchased the book, Bessie hadn't given it much thought. Maybe what she was feeling had something to do with the second author. Sighing, she stood up and stretched. It was dark outside, so too late for another walk on the beach, but it was clear, which made it a good night for sitting on the rock behind her cottage.

Bessie pulled on a heavy coat and comfortable shoes and then let herself out of the cottage's back door. The tide was out far enough that she was able to easily walk to the rock, which was wide enough for two people to sit on comfortably. The sky seemed full of stars, and Bessie felt her mood improving as she breathed in sea air and stared at the waves and the heavens. She'd lost track of time when a noise from somewhere behind her made her jump.

Turning around, she looked at the cottages along the beach. The only one that had any lights on inside was Andrew's, which was as it should have been. The sound seemed to have come from further away, though. The stars and the nearly full moon did their best to illuminate the night for Bessie. Movement caught her eye.

Something or someone was definitely moving near the last cottage, she realised. She was off the rock and halfway to the cottage before her brain caught up with her feet. If someone was attempting to break into the last cottage, confronting that someone could be dangerous. Bessie's mobile phone was on the counter in her kitchen, plugged into its charger. As she hesitated, wondering what to do next, she saw someone walk through the cottage.

Stepping backwards, into the shadow of the neighbouring cottage, Bessie watched intently as the intruder slowly disappeared down the corridor, presumably heading for one of the bedrooms. Her heart raced as she counted to one hundred. Nothing moved inside the cottage. She was halfway to a hundred the second time when she got bored and stopped. After looking up and down the beach and seeing no one, she slowly walked up to the sliding door at the back of the cottage.

She cautiously crept up the steps to the door and then peered through the glass. It was dark and difficult to see, but she was certain the room wasn't empty. She tested the door and found it locked before she made her way back down the stairs as quietly as she could.

Someone is clearly staying in the cottage, she thought as she reached the sand. Feeling slightly safer back on the beach, she slowly walked all the way around the cottage, but couldn't see anything amiss. Knowing that there was someone inside kept her from peering into the bedroom windows. After her circuit, she stood behind the cottage and tried to decide what to do next. The wind began to pick up as she paced back and forth. Shivering, she decided to do her thinking from inside her kitchen.

As she walked towards Andrew's cottage, the only light she could see was in one of the bedrooms. It switched off suddenly as she approached.

"I don't want to disturb him," she muttered to herself as she continued on towards home. *Of course, by now, whoever is in the last cottage is probably asleep, as well,* she thought as she let herself back inside. *Really, it would be a shame to wake him or her.* The more she thought about it, the more Bessie felt that there was little harm in leaving the intruder alone for the night. She'd check the cottage again in the morning and, if she could see anything inside, she'd ring the police immediately, she decided.

Feeling only slightly uneasy about the decision, Bessie

chose another book at random from her pile of new titles and then headed up the stairs to get ready for bed. She managed only a single chapter before she found that she couldn't keep her eyes open any longer. Yawning, she switched off the light and slid under the covers. *I'll never sleep, knowing someone has broken into the last cottage,* was her last conscious thought before six.

* * *

WHEN BESSIE OPENED HER EYES, the intruder was the first thing that came to mind. Hurrying through her shower, she decided to skip breakfast in favour of a very early morning walk. As the sun wasn't up yet, she picked up a torch and slipped it into her coat pocket. It was still overcast and windy, and Bessie found herself questioning her sanity when a light rain began to fall.

As she approached the last cottage, she began to look for footprints, but the wind and the rain seemed to have obscured even the ones that she knew should have been there.

"Hello?" she called in a low voice as she approached the sliding door. "If you're going to call, you need to shout," she muttered to herself. "Hello?" she said as she climbed the steps, speaking only slightly more loudly than before.

Switching on her torch, she shined it into the cottage. It was completely empty, just as it should be. Bessie felt as if she should rub her eyes and look again. She'd been certain she had seen a bag and maybe a pair of shoes on the floor in the room the previous evening. Was it possible that her eyes had been playing tricks on her in the dark?

Maybe I didn't really see a person in the cottage, either, she thought as she slowly walked back down the steps to the beach. Feeling grateful that she hadn't rung the police, Bessie walked around the cottage, looking into every window. There was no sign that anyone had been there, and the windows were all shut and locked, just as they should have been.

Sighing, Bessie slipped the torch back into her pocket and continued along the beach. When she reached the stairs to Thie yn Traie, she decided to turn around. It was still dark, it was cold, and it was raining. She'd take another walk later, when it would at least be lighter.

Back at home, she made tea and toast and then picked up the book she'd discarded the previous evening. She was struggling through another chapter when someone knocked on her door a short while later.

"Good morning," Andrew said when she'd opened the door. "I woke up early and couldn't get back to sleep. Have you already had your walk on the beach this morning?"

"I have, and it's a bit cold and wet for another one, I think," Bessie said, glancing up at the sky. "Why don't you come in and have a cuppa?"

"That's the best offer I've had all day," he laughed as he walked into the kitchen. "But you were reading. I've interrupted."

"You're welcome to interrupt that book. I'm not enjoying it."

"No?"

"I don't know if it's just me or if it's because the author worked with another author on this title, but the characters just don't feel the same."

"Does that mean you'll be happy to take me sightseeing today, then?" Andrew asked.

"I'm always happy to do that, even if I'm in the middle of a good book. But I thought you'd seen most of the island's sights by now."

He nodded. "I have, but some of them are certainly worth

a second look. I thought maybe we could go around Castle Rushen again and then have lunch in Castletown."

"That would be a good plan, except Castle Rushen is shut at the moment. Manx National Heritage is starting to get it ready for Christmas at the Castle," Bessie told him.

"In that case, what would you suggest for today?" he asked.

The ringing of her telephone kept Bessie from having to think of a reply.

"It's Mark Blake," the voice on the other end of the receiver said. "I know this is last-minute and you have your friend visiting, but I could really use an hour of your time at the castle this morning. The committee needs to make a few decisions about which rooms to use and how to arrange things this year, and none of the other committee members are available."

"I didn't realise we were changing anything from last year," Bessie replied.

"We weren't going to, but then the roof began to leak in three places," Mark explained. "The leaks have all been patched, but we can't use the rooms that have been affected until proper repairs can be done in the spring. We're going to have to reroute traffic through the castle, and we're going to have to use some different areas than we usually do."

Bessie sighed. "That's the price we pay for using a medieval castle, isn't it?"

Mark laughed. "Maybe next year we should have the entire event in a brand new building somewhere."

"But this is serendipitous, as my friend was just saying he wanted to visit Castle Rushen today. I assume you don't mind if he has a little wander around while we talk."

"He'll be more than welcome to take himself around the castle or to join us as we walk through and talk about options," Mark assured her. "If he has a car, I can meet you both there in an hour. Otherwise, I'll collect you from Treoghe Bwaane in forty minutes or so."

"He does have a car. We'll see you in Castletown in an hour."

She put the phone down and grinned at Andrew. "How about a private tour of Castle Rushen?" she asked.

"I couldn't ask for more," he replied.

Mark insisted on buying them lunch after they'd finished touring the castle and choosing the rooms for the upcoming event.

"I hope you don't mind having lunch at the café at the Manx Museum," Mark said as he walked them to Andrew's car. "I need to get back to Douglas."

After lunch, Bessie took Andrew around the museum, even though he'd toured it before. She tried to point out things he might have missed on his previous visits. It was nearly five o'clock by the time they headed back to Laxey.

"I'm hoping for a nice long email from Jeff," Andrew told Bessie as he drove. "And I'm hoping he answered all of our questions."

"Including who killed Paul Bernhard," Bessie suggested.

"Yes, well, it might be a bit optimistic, hoping for an answer to that one."

He left Bessie at her cottage and walked back to his own to check his email. With her friends due to arrive in fifteen minutes, Bessie quickly ran the vacuum through the ground-floor rooms. No matter how careful she tried to be, sand always seemed to be everywhere in the cottage. She was just putting the vacuum away when someone knocked on the door.

CHAPTER 10

"*I* was afraid I was going to be late," Hugh said after Bessie had given him a hug.

"And instead, you're first," she replied.

He shrugged. "I didn't have far to come, but I got a bit caught up playing with the baby and lost track of time."

"How is the baby?" Bessie asked.

"She's doing so much now, walking a little bit and pointing and babbling and...." He trailed off and gave Bessie a smile. "She's amazing, and I can't quite believe that she's ours. I'm trying hard to enjoy every minute I'm with her because I'm told that she won't want to spend so much time with me when she's a teenager."

"That's when she'll start spending her time here," Bessie suggested.

Hugh laughed. "I won't mind if she does, but I hope she doesn't feel as if she needs to come here to get away from her life at home."

"I'm certain that you and Grace are doing an amazing job with her. She'll always be welcome here, of course, whatever the circumstances."

John and Doona arrived with the food a moment later. As Bessie let them in, she noticed Andrew locking the door to his cottage. He waved as he crossed the beach towards her.

"I'm sorry I'm late," he told everyone as Bessie shut the door behind him. "I wanted to send Harry and Charles an update based on the email that I received from Jeff."

"What have you learned?" Bessie asked eagerly.

"Let's get food first," he suggested. "I can't believe it, but I'm actually starving again."

"It's the sea air," John told him. "When I first moved here, I found myself eating almost constantly. You do get used to it after a while."

"I'm not so sure about that," Hugh said.

Everyone laughed, and then Bessie got down plates while Doona laid out the food that she and John had brought.

"Pizza?" Hugh asked as Doona began to open boxes. "Is it from the new place across from the station?"

Doona nodded. "We've heard good and bad things about it, but we haven't tried it yet," she told him. "It just opened a few days ago, after all."

"I took pizza home from there yesterday," Hugh told her. "I got one with just cheese and one with everything. It was like the two pizzas had come from completely different restaurants. The crusts were different, the sauces were different and only one of them was edible."

"Which one?" Bessie asked, eyeing up the three options in front of her.

"The one with just cheese," he told her.

Bessie took a slice of the pizza with just cheese and then a piece of garlic bread. "This looks good, anyway," she said of the crusty bread slice that appeared to have been liberally spread with garlic butter.

"The garlic bread was good," Hugh told her. "I was happy

I'd added it to the order, since we didn't eat one of the pizzas."

John went into the dining room and brought back a chair, shifting the four around the kitchen table to make room for it. Doona got cold drinks for everyone. A few minutes later, they all sat down together around the table.

"It's good," Bessie said after her first bite. "Not the best pizza I've ever had, but not the worst, by far."

Hugh nodded. "It's the same as the one we had last night," he told her. "Unfortunately, the one with everything looks the same, too."

Doona took a bite and made a face. "The crust is like cardboard," she said. "And the sauce is bitter."

"I don't understand why they don't use the same crust and sauce for all of their pizzas," Bessie said.

"I'm afraid to suggest it," Hugh told her. "What if they start making all of their pizzas like the one with everything?"

Doona made a face. "It's a good thing we brought a lot more than we thought we were going to need." She went back to the counter and got herself a couple of slices of the pizza with just cheese. When she'd sat back down, Andrew cleared his throat.

"I've had some information back from Jeff," he said. "And I've brought us something to do after dinner." He waved towards the bag he'd left on the counter.

"What have you brought?" Bessie asked.

"Let's talk about what I've heard first," he suggested. "I told him that Charles knows someone who might be able to narrow down the location from which Maria was allegedly writing her emails. He was, well, let's say surprised to hear that someone in the UK might know New York City better than he does, but he also said he'd be delighted if Charles's friend could find Maria."

"It doesn't sound as if he thinks that's very likely," John remarked.

"But he's open to all possibilities. This case has been bothering him for over a year now. He'll be thrilled if we manage to suggest something that actually helps solve it," Andrew replied.

"What else did he have to say?" Doona asked as Andrew stopped to take a bite of garlic bread.

"He thought Harry's idea of trying to attract Maria, or whoever was behind the emails from Maria, by joining similar newsgroups was a good one. It was something he'd considered, but he simply doesn't have the time to join several groups and try to stay on top of them all. He did point out, though, that there are hundreds or even thousands of newsgroups and that it may be impossible to find the right person or people," Andrew told her.

"If it truly is a gang of people, though, they may have people hanging around on many different groups," Hugh said. "Harry may find himself making lots of new friends."

Andrew nodded. "Harry is going to forward anything he gets to me, and I'll make copies for everyone. We want to watch for any approach that feels similar to the way that Maria started things with Paul."

"Pudding?" Hugh asked hopefully as he finished his last bite of pizza.

"We brought a strawberry and rhubarb pie from the bakery in Ramsey," Doona told him. "And one of their chocolate cream pies, as well."

Hugh's eyes lit up. "Let me help," he said, getting to his feet. He began clearing away plates, tipping half-eaten pieces of pizza into the bin as he went.

"I'm going to throw away the nasty pizza," Doona told them. "There are a few slices of just cheese and of ham and mushroom, which seems to be the same as the cheese one, if anyone wants more."

"John, take what's left home to the children," Bessie suggested as everyone refused.

"I will, only because Thomas is always looking for a snack around midnight. He'll be delighted to have leftover pizza," John told her.

Hugh did the washing-up while Doona sliced into the pies. Everyone got a slice of his or her favourite, and Hugh got a slice of each.

"Where were we?" Andrew asked after his first bite of the fruit pie.

"You were telling us what Jeff had to say," Bessie told him before taking a bite of the delicious chocolate option.

"I believe that Jeff tends to agree with John that the men working on the site should have been questioned more thoroughly at the time," Andrew replied. "He's going to go back and try to speak to each of them again, focussing on whether or not any of them knew Leon or Max, and also finding out if any of them have ever played Prisoners of Cardavar."

"I'll be very interested in hearing what he learns," John said.

"And that just leaves us with Leon and Max," Andrew concluded. "Jeff rang a few people and discovered that they're both back in Germany now. He's going to speak to a contact he has in Berlin and see if they can each be questioned, at least informally, again."

Bessie frowned. "Why informally?"

"Lacking any new information, Jeff can't request that they be taken in for formal questioning. He had a chance to speak to them himself when they were living in New York, after all. He's going to be relying on cooperation from the German police now. I suspect they'll be happy to help as much as they can, seeing as how the victim was also German, but it's a more complicated situation than speaking to, say, the workers from the site," Andrew explained.

"Would it be easier for you to speak to them?" Bessie asked.

"I'd need to get all sorts of clearances and permissions," Andrew sighed.

"Maybe I need to take a trip to Berlin," Bessie muttered. "There aren't any rules about me talking to people I meet on my travels."

Andrew cleared his throat. "Actually, as a part of this team, you can't go and speak to any of the witnesses in the cases we're discussing, not without clearance through Scotland Yard."

Bessie stared at him for a minute, temporarily speechless. "Scotland Yard?" she said eventually.

"That is who you're working for, ultimately," Andrew told her.

Sitting back in her chair, Bessie took a deep breath. While she'd known that Andrew had worked for Scotland Yard, and she knew that he'd made some sort of arrangements with someone to set up the unit in the first place, she hadn't actually considered that she was working for Scotland Yard.

"While Bessie thinks about that, what else do we need to discuss?" Doona asked, an amused look on her face.

"I think that was about all that Jeff had to say for the moment," Andrew replied. "He'll be emailing me daily, keeping me informed as to what else he discovers."

"Did you say you'd brought something else for us to do?" Hugh asked around a mouthful of pie.

"Don't talk with your mouth full," Bessie said automatically, her mind still processing Andrew's earlier remark.

Andrew laughed. "I did bring something for us to do," he agreed. "I thought it might be interesting to take a look at Prisoners of Cardavar."

He walked over to the counter and picked up the bag he'd left there. When he'd sat back down, he pulled out a large box. Bessie recognised it as something he'd purchased at the toyshop earlier in the day. At the time, she hadn't paid attention to what he was buying.

"That's a lot more sophisticated than the set I had a few years back," Hugh said as Andrew removed the plastic wrapping from the box. "I just had a book and a few pairs of dice."

"The shop assistant told me that this was the complete set, whatever that means," Andrew replied. He opened the box and set it in the middle of the table.

Bessie stared at the many different dice, each one nestled in its own plastic section.

"How many sides can there be on a die?" she asked as she pulled a red one out of the box.

"There are different dice for different things," Hugh explained. "The largest has twenty sides, but you'll use the twelve-sided and some of the regular, six-sided dice for most turns."

"I don't think I'm going to understand this," Bessie sighed.

"There's a book," Andrew said, lifting the plastic tray full of dice out of the box.

"It's an encyclopedia." Bessie gasped at the thick hard-cover book.

Andrew nodded. "I don't think we have time to read through it tonight."

"Most of it is reference tables and charts," Hugh told him. "The actual rules of the game are pretty simple."

"Are they?" Andrew asked dryly as he opened the book. He flipped through it for a moment and then looked up at Hugh. "There are twenty-four pages of rules," he said.

"If you just want to get a feel for how the game works, I can walk you through it," Hugh offered. "Are there player sheets in the box?"

Andrew lifted up a card that said "Quick Start Instructions" across the top and then pulled out a thick pad of paper.

"Everyone needs a player sheet," Hugh told him.

Andrew tore off sheets and passed one to each of them.

"I don't really want..." Bessie began.

"We should all understand the basics," Andrew argued. "We won't play for long and, anyway, you'll get bored if you just sit there and watch us."

Feeling as if watching couldn't be any more boring than playing, Bessie took the sheet and stared at the rows and columns. The headings were all groups of letters and numbers and none of it made any sense to her.

Hugh took all of the different dice out of the tray and put them in the centre of the table.

"We even got pencils," Andrew said, passing around short pencils with "Prisoners of Cardavar" stamped along them in tiny print.

"Everyone needs to start by developing a character," Hugh told them. "You can choose a name, but everything else depends on rolling the various dice."

"Choose a name?" Bessie echoed.

"Yes, pick something you like, maybe something that sounds powerful," he suggested. "It goes in the box at the very top of the player card."

Bessie thought about it for a moment and then wrote "Bessie" on her card. Andrew looked over and chuckled. He wrote "Alexander the Great" on his sheet.

"If everyone has a name, we can start establishing our characters," Hugh said. "Bessie, why don't you go first? Start with the largest die. You're going to roll each die a single time. Mark what you get on your sheet and then we'll work out what it means."

Sighing, Bessie picked up the largest die and rolled it.

Andrew showed her where to mark what she'd rolled on her sheet. A minute later she'd rolled all of the dice, both large and small. She sighed again as she passed the dice along to Andrew. When everyone had finished rolling and marking their results, Hugh opened the book and began to flip through it.

"We can start with me," he said. "My character, um, Xavier, has average intelligence and above-average strength. He's taller than average, but also slightly overweight. He has a sword, and one magic potion that can restore health or create a bridge across an otherwise insurmountable obstacle."

"That's some potion," Bessie muttered.

Hugh went around the table, informing each player of his or her characteristics. By the time he reached Bessie, she was longing to get back to the book that she'd disliked so much.

"Bessie, your character, er, Bessie, is short and thin, but, in terms of intelligence, you're brilliant. You rolled the highest possible intelligence score and then rolled a super boost to give you an unbeatable level of brilliance. You also possess the book of knowledge and the potion of problem-solving," Hugh told her.

Everyone around the table laughed. "The game knows Bessie as well as we do," Doona said.

"It was just dumb luck," Bessie muttered.

"Or brilliant luck, as the case may be," Hugh countered.

"What now?" Andrew asked.

"Now we begin to play," Hugh told him. "According to the story, we're all from other places in the universe, sent to Cardavar for crimes we may or may not have committed. We'll roll for that later in the game."

"Of course we will," Bessie said softly.

Andrew patted her arm. "If you win, you can have what's left of the chocolate pie," he told her.

Suddenly tempted to get herself another slice, Bessie shifted in her seat. "Maybe I should make tea," she suggested. "It seems as if this could take a while."

"We won't finish tonight," Hugh said. "I mean, we can, if we want to take shortcuts. If you want to play the full game, though, it takes at least six or seven hours."

Bessie stared at him, speechless for the second time that evening. "Six or seven hours?" she repeated. "Who spends that sort of time on a game?"

Hugh shrugged. "People who enjoy the game. I have some friends who really got into it for a while. It can actually be quite challenging and interesting to play. I have one friend who's been playing a similar game with a group of friends from school. They've been playing the same game for three years."

"That's dedication," Doona said.

"Prisoners of Cardavar is different, though," Hugh added. "It's meant to have an end, where some role-playing games don't necessarily. In Prisoners of Cardavar, you have one single goal and once you accomplish that, you're finished."

"What's the goal?" John asked.

"Escaping from Cardavar," Hugh replied.

"I think we should at least start," Andrew said. "I've read the emails between Paul and Maria several times and their references to the game confuse me. I'd really like to understand what they're talking about."

Bessie nodded. "I know what you mean," she said, getting to her feet. "But if we are going to try this, I'm going to need tea."

"I don't suppose you have any wine," Doona muttered.

Bessie laughed. "I wish I did."

"Right," Hugh said a few minutes later, after Bessie had passed around tea and biscuits. "The person with the highest health power goes first. That's John."

"What do I do?" John asked.

"Roll the green and the small black dice," Hugh told him. He flipped through the book. "What can happen on your first turn is different to later turns. Go ahead and roll."

John threw the dice onto the table. "One and four," he told Hugh.

Hugh spent a moment looking at the charts and tables and then began to laugh.

"What's so funny?" John asked after a moment. "Don't tell me I'm dead already."

Bessie was quite certain that she hadn't imagined that John sounded somewhat hopeful that his character might have died on his first turn.

"No, you aren't dead. According to this, it's been discovered that you were sent to Cardavar in error. You need to roll the white die. If you get an even number, you become a prison guard. If you get an odd number, you get promoted to head guard."

Everyone around the table laughed as John threw a three and was promptly promoted to head guard in the prison.

An hour later, Bessie had had enough. While she was beginning to understand the appeal of the game, the randomness of the roll of the dice was starting to really annoy her.

"I'm sorry, but someone else is going to have to keep playing for me, if I can't simply drop out," she said before her next turn.

"I think we can stop there for tonight," Andrew said. "I've a much better understanding of how the game works. There are definitely some things said in the later emails that are game references."

"I noticed that, but I didn't think it made much difference," Hugh said.

Andrew nodded. "Having tried the game now, I'm inclined to agree with you. I was rather hoping for more."

Hugh collected all of the character sheets and then repacked the box. "We can resume any time," he told them as he handed the box to Andrew.

"Maybe not," Doona suggested.

"Just because you're in solitary confinement because you started a fight doesn't mean you can't still win," Hugh told her.

"That's good to know," Doona replied sarcastically.

"Thank you for your help," Andrew told Hugh. "I do think tonight's exercise was useful, even if nothing comes of it. I'll be reading through the emails again when I get back to my cottage, just in case I missed something, though."

Everyone helped with the washing-up and tidying of the kitchen, and it wasn't long before Bessie found herself on her own. It was too early to go to bed, so she got out the case file and read back through the emails.

She was surprised to find that she did understand a great many more of the game references that Paul and Maria had used throughout their conversation, but when she was done she didn't feel as if her new knowledge had brought her any closer to finding Paul's killer.

CHAPTER 11

fter such an unusual evening, Bessie found herself pacing around the kitchen as the clock ticked past her bedtime. Feeling as if she should have discussed what she'd seen at the last cottage with John and Andrew, she was now faced with having to make a decision as to what she wanted to do about the situation. After arguing with herself for several minutes, she sat down and wrote a note.

I'm sure you know that you're trespassing on private property by staying here. I don't want to have you arrested. There may be some way that I can help. Please meet me on the rock behind my cottage tomorrow evening at ten. Miss Elizabeth Cubbon, Treoghe Bwaane, Laxey.

It wasn't perfect, but she was too tired to think of a better way to say what she wanted to say. She slipped the note into an envelope and then pulled on her coat and shoes and grabbed her torch. Andrew's cottage was already dark, as were the rest of the cottages in the row. As she approached the last cottage, she started listening carefully for sounds of movement.

The marks in the sand that she could see by the light of

her torch weren't exactly footprints. It looked more as if something had been dragged through the sand. *Perhaps someone had been trying to hide footprints,* Bessie thought. The sliding door was shut as Bessie approached, so she didn't even bother climbing the stairs. Instead, she began a slow walk around the house, looking for an open window.

She found one at the front of the property, facing the car park and the road that no one would be using at this time of year. A window in one of the bedrooms was open just an inch, maybe less. Bessie dropped her note though the window and then walked briskly back home. As she locked her door behind herself, she began to worry about what she'd done.

"What if there isn't anyone there?" she asked her reflection as she washed her face. "Maggie will find the note and think that I've lost my mind. She'll ring John, and he'll think the same thing."

Shaking her head at her foolishness, Bessie got into bed and pulled the covers up to her chin. In the morning, she'd ring Maggie and tell her everything, she decided. That was the safest option.

* * *

HER SLEEP WAS RESTLESS, and she was happy to get up at six and start her day. Of course, it was far too early to ring Maggie, but that would be her first job once it reached a reasonable hour. She made herself porridge for breakfast, mostly as a punishment. She hated porridge, but she knew it was good for her so she tried to eat it at least once a week. Today, though, she felt as if she deserved porridge.

"It was an impulse," she muttered as she put on her coat and shoes, ready for her morning walk. "Whoever is breaking in is being very careful and keeping the cottage clean. He or she may have fallen on difficult times. I simply wanted to help."

Outside, she marched rapidly down the beach, ignoring the holiday cottages as she went. By keeping her eyes firmly fixed on the sea, she managed to walk some distance past Thie yn Traie without actually noticing how far she'd gone. As a light rain began to fall, she turned for home.

When she opened her door and stepped inside, Bessie's heart skipped a beat. On the kitchen table, there was a small white envelope that hadn't been there when she'd gone out.

"Hello?" she called anxiously, holding her breath and listening for a reply. "Hello?" she repeated a moment later. The cottage was silent.

The voice in her head was shouting at her to ring the police as Bessie pushed her door shut. She'd just read the note and then ring the police, she thought as she crossed the room.

Miss Elizabeth Cubbon had been neatly printed on the front of the envelope. Bessie guessed that it was the same envelope that she'd used the previous evening. The sheet inside was definitely the same, with the reply written on the back of her note, in the same careful printing.

Thank you. I could use some help. I'll see you at ten.

Bessie read the words several times. While it was tempting to ring John, that wouldn't be fair to the person who'd written the note. She was still wondering what to do when the phone rang.

"Hello?"

"Bessie, it's Andy, Andy Caine. How are you?"

"Andy? My goodness, I thought maybe you'd left the island. It's been ages since I've seen you."

"I have been off-island, actually, but I'm back now."

"And we're overdue for a good long conversation. Let's

have lunch tomorrow," Bessie suggested. "We could go to the café in Lonan."

"Tomorrow?"

"Is that not enough notice? I can do the next day, if you'd prefer."

"No, tomorrow is fine," Andy said after a moment. "What did you want to talk with me about?"

"Let's save that for tomorrow around midday, shall we?"

Andy sighed. "Yeah, okay," he muttered before he ended the call.

"Something else about which I will worry," Bessie said as she put the receiver down. "He didn't sound at all happy."

She was pacing around the kitchen, worrying about half a dozen different things when Andrew knocked.

"Let's go and get lunch somewhere," he suggested when she opened the door.

Bessie looked at the clock. "It's only nine o'clock."

"Yes, but if we drive halfway around the island, it will be closer to time for lunch."

"Maybe half nine, even," Bessie suggested.

Andrew laughed. "Okay, I know it's a small island, but I'm feeling restless this morning. All of this waiting to hear back from Jeff is starting to get to me. What I really want to do is fly to Berlin and question Leon and Max. If nothing else, I'd like to learn more about Paul."

"I don't feel as if I know anything about him," Bessie said with a sigh.

"That was one of the reasons why I wanted to try that game last night. It seems to have been one of his hobbies, really the only one about which we know."

"I'm still not sure about why he was in New York. From what we do know of his life, he doesn't seem the sort who would do something impulsive. And flying halfway around the world to meet someone you don't know, after just a few emails, is incredibly impulsive."

Andrew nodded. "You're right, of course. More questions for Leon and Max, I think."

"He had a fiancée, as well," Bessie added. "Had he cheated on her before? Was he the sort that always cheated on partners? His friends from home should know the answers to those questions."

"I'm going to send another quick email to Jeff," Andrew said. "With the time difference, he's probably still in bed. If he hasn't spoken to Max or Leon yet, hopefully he can add a few questions to the ones he's planning to ask them."

"He might ask Anja a few questions, too," Bessie suggested.

Andrew nodded and rushed out, leaving Bessie wondering about their plans for the day. She was just flipping through a book, not really reading it, when he returned.

"Now let's go somewhere for lunch," he said with a rueful grin.

"We're meeting everyone at two, aren't we?" Bessie asked.

"We are, although I don't know that we'll have anything to discuss."

"You'll want to check your laptop again just before the meeting, won't you?" Bessie asked.

"I will, yes, although I can take it with us and check it from the Seaview. Jasper told me that they can accommodate that."

"So where do you want to go now?" Bessie asked.

"Douglas," Andrew decided. "We can stroll around the shops and get lunch at that Italian place that does the amazing garlic bread. I know I just had garlic bread last night, but it wasn't the same."

"I'm not going to argue with that," Bessie laughed.

The city centre was reasonably quiet, and the pair

enjoyed their time strolling around the shops. Bessie treated herself to a box of chocolates, and Andrew bought some socks, as he'd discovered that morning that he hadn't packed enough pairs for his stay. Lunch was every bit as delicious as they'd hoped, and they were on their way back to Laxey with time to spare.

They stopped at Andrew's cottage so that he could check his emails and then headed for the Seaview. Hugh was already in the conference room when they arrived. He was sitting at the table with a book open in front of him, taking notes in a notebook.

"Oh, is it time?" he asked, jumping up and beginning to gather up his things.

"We're a few minutes early," Andrew told him. "What are you studying?"

"Maths," Hugh replied, making a face. "It's not that difficult. It just takes time to get through the homework, that's all. I worked only a half day today because of the meeting, so I thought I could come here and get some homework done while I waited."

"That was a good idea," Andrew told him. "Did you get much done?"

"Probably half of what's due tomorrow night. I'll do the rest after the meeting. Maybe I'll ask Jasper if he has a quiet corner where I could work."

"The baby doesn't let you do much at home, then?" Bessie guessed.

"Actually, she's very good about leaving me alone when I'm working. I'm just not very good about not wanting to play with her when I'm there," Hugh admitted. "Besides, I feel guilty that Grace has to do everything for Aalish every day. When I'm home, I feel as if I should do it all, even when I should be doing homework."

"I can't see Jasper minding if you stay in here after the

meeting," Andrew said. "I doubt very much that they'll have another group waiting to use the room."

John and Doona arrived a moment later, and Charles wasn't far behind them. Jasper had put out a lavish tea with finger sandwiches, cream cakes, and piles of other treats. Everyone filled plates and then settled in around the table. Harry strolled in, just a few minutes late. He nodded at everyone and then took a seat.

"Do you want anything to eat or drink?" Andrew asked him.

"No, thanks," he replied.

"Unfortunately, I don't have much to report," Andrew began. "Jeff has been doing his best, but thus far he hasn't had much success with even finding the people we've requested he interview again. Before I get to that, though, do any of you have anything to report?"

"My friend in New York is certain he knows which building Maria was living in when she sent her emails," Charles said, sounding slightly smug to Bessie.

"What's the address?" Andrew asked.

Charles shrugged. "I didn't ask him that. He has it and he's going to go and talk to a few people in the building. He expects that he'll be able to find Maria by the end of the day today."

"That's very optimistic," Harry said.

"He's very good," Charles shot back.

"You're assuming that Maria actually exists and that she actually lived in New York," Harry replied. "I don't believe either of those things are true."

"You may believe what you like," Charles told him.

"If he does find Maria, he'll need to inform Jeff immediately. He isn't to try to question the woman himself," Andrew said.

Charles nodded. "I've told him that. He knows he's simply

meant to find her. As I said, he's very good. People talk to him, and he knows New York the way that I know London. He probably knows someone with connections to that building. He'll get a full list of everyone named Maria who ever lived in that building, anyway."

"And that will be helpful," Harry muttered sarcastically.

"At least I'm making progress," Charles said tightly. "I've not been sitting around playing games."

Harry laughed. "My gameplay has a serious purpose. I'm trying to find the people who pretended to be Maria, the ones who got Paul to come to New York for reasons we've yet to determine."

"How is that going?" Andrew asked.

"It's been interesting," Harry replied. "I've been active on six different role-playing game newsgroups, and I've had more than a dozen private messages from other players. Most of them have been very specifically about the game, but a few have been more general. One was from someone claiming to be a young woman who has only recently started playing and is hoping to make some friends in real life through the game."

"And you're replying to some of them?" Hugh wondered.

"I'm replying to all of them," Harry told him. "Obviously, I put more time and effort into the reply to the young woman than any of the others, as her approach is the most similar to Maria's, but I'm not ruling anyone out yet."

"Has anyone suggested a meeting yet?" Andrew asked.

"I've been invited to games in both Birmingham and Glasgow. I've told everyone I'm in London, by the way. I've also had one person, claiming to be a woman, hint that she might enjoy talking dirty, shall we say? I'm playing dumb for the moment, but we'll see how that develops. The young woman who's looking for friends hasn't replied to me yet."

"If nothing else, I'm fascinated by what you're doing," Andrew told him. "Keep me informed."

Harry nodded. "I don't know if anyone I've met has any connection to Paul, but I'm pretty certain at least a few of them have criminal intent."

"The rest of us met last night and spent some time playing Prisoners of Cardavar," Andrew told Harry and Charles. "It was interesting to try out the game, but I don't think we learned anything that will help with the investigation."

"If you do it again, let me know," Harry said. "I'm doing my best, pretending to be a player, but I've never actually even seen the game. I'm getting everything off the Internet, which isn't always the most reliable place to find things."

"I have the game in my boot," Andrew told him. "I'm more than happy to let you borrow it if you want to take a look."

"Yes, please. If anyone has the time, I'd quite like to try a game, actually," Harry said, looking around the table.

Bessie looked down at her empty biscuit plate, determined not to look back up until someone had changed the subject.

"I can spare an hour later today," Doona said eventually. "I'll come back to the Seaview around five, if that works for you. I'll see if I can persuade Thomas or Amy to come, as well."

Harry nodded at her. "I rarely say this, but the more people, the better."

"Unfortunately, Bessie and I have plans for this evening," Andrew said. "If there's nothing else for today, let's meet again the day after tomorrow. That should give Jeff time to question a few people, give Charles's associate time to find Maria, and give Harry time to hear back from some of his new friends."

The others were quick to agree. Bessie took her time gathering her things while Andrew went out to his car to get the game for Harry. As the group began to disperse, Bessie caught Doona's arm.

"I can't believe you're going to play that game again voluntarily," she whispered.

Doona shrugged. "In a weird way, it was almost fun, getting to be someone else and letting the roll of a die decide my fate. Besides, it may help Harry with the investigation."

Hugh was getting his maths textbook out as Doona left the room. Andrew walked back into the room, frowning.

"I should have offered to play with them this afternoon," he told Bessie.

"But we have plans," she replied.

He laughed. "We do now, anyway. I don't know what they are, but they definitely don't include Prisoners of Cardavar."

"Good luck with the homework," Bessie told Hugh as she and Andrew walked towards the door.

"Thanks," he muttered, clearly focussed on the book in front of him.

Jasper was in the corridor. "Was everything satisfactory?" he asked.

"Of course," Bessie told him. "Hugh is just finishing up some maths homework. If he's in the way, just let him know."

"He's more than welcome to sit there all afternoon," Jasper laughed. "I'll send in one of my catering staff to start clearing up, but if he disturbs Hugh, he can do it later. We don't need the room again until next month."

"We are meeting again," Andrew said quickly.

"I know. I have you scheduled for a conference room the day after tomorrow, but I thought I would put you in a different room. I meant to move you this time, but I forgot to change it on the master schedule. Anyway, next time you'll be meeting in the room on the first floor. That should keep Dan Ross from noticing."

Bessie grinned at him. "Very good."

"I hope I remember to tell everyone," Andrew said.

"I'll help you remember," Bessie promised.

Jasper escorted them through the hotel and into the enormous lobby. "Thank you again for choosing the Seaview," he told Andrew.

"It's my pleasure," Andrew replied.

As he and Bessie got back into Andrew's car, he glanced at her. "What are our plans, then?" he asked.

"We had lunch in Douglas. What about dinner in Peel?" she asked.

"Peel? Why not?"

"We could drive over now and stroll around the House of Manannan for an hour before getting something to eat at one of the pubs near there," Bessie suggested.

"I did want to visit the House of Manannan again, actually. There was so much to see that I'm certain I missed a great deal."

"We may not have time to do the entire museum, but I've been through it often enough to take you through and make sure you see the best parts."

After a drive across the centre of the island and a short tour of the museum, Andrew drove them to a nearby pub.

Bessie ordered cottage pie. "This is terribly indulgent after our huge lunch," she commented as the waiter walked away.

"As long as we don't do this every day, we'll be fine," Andrew replied. "When I'm at home in London, I eat much more sensibly."

"As do I, when I'm not caught up in a murder investigation."

They chatted about the weather and British politics while they waited for their food.

"Delicious," Bessie said when she'd finished. She pushed

her empty plate away and sighed. "I wish I had room for pudding. They do wonderful Victoria sponge here."

"Anything else?" the waiter asked as he cleared their plates.

"Two slices of Victoria sponge to take away," Andrew told him, winking at Bessie.

As they drove back across the island, their puddings safely tucked away in the boot, Bessie thought about her plans for the evening ahead. While Andrew parked his car, she decided that she needed to tell him what she'd done.

"And that's why I'm going to be meeting someone at ten o'clock tonight," she concluded a short while later.

"This someone could be dangerous."

"Or he or she could simply be in some sort of trouble. Whoever it is has been very careful about leaving the cottage neat and tidy."

"But whoever it is obviously has great skill with opening locks," Andrew pointed out. "What if he or she has simply agreed to the meeting to distract you? You'll be out on your rock while he or she is in here, stealing everything of value that you own."

"Which isn't much," Bessie replied. "Anyway, I thought maybe you could sit in here while I'm out on the rock. If you switch off the lights inside the cottage, you should be able to see the rock and keep an eye on me."

"Assuming the weather cooperates," Andrew muttered.

CHAPTER 12

Of course, the weather didn't want to cooperate. With five minutes to go before the meeting, Andrew was doing everything he could to persuade Bessie not to go.

"It's raining and dark. I won't be able to see anything out there. You could be putting yourself in great danger."

"I never should have told you about the meeting," she countered. "If I hadn't mentioned it, you'd be fast asleep right now."

"I'm coming with you, then."

"You can't. This person doesn't trust me yet. He or she certainly isn't going to trust me if I bring a Scotland Yard inspector along to our first meeting."

Andrew sighed deeply and then shrugged. "If I can't change your mind, then I'll sit here in the dark and hope I'll be able to at least see something."

"I'm going to take a torch. You'll be able to see that."

Andrew nodded.

A moment later, she put on her shoes and her thickest raincoat. She found an umbrella and slid her torch into her pocket. "Here goes nothing," she muttered as she headed for the door. As she went out, she switched off the lights, leaving Andrew sitting at the kitchen table in the dark.

Putting up the umbrella and switching on the torch, Bessie took a few steps towards the rock and then sighed. The wind was blowing the rain sidewise, which made the umbrella both useless and awkward to hold. Shutting it, she continued down the beach, waving her torch back and forth as she went, more for Andrew's benefit than her own.

She settled on the rock sideways so that she could watch for anyone who might approach. Fifteen minutes later, she was soaked through and ready to give up. As she started to try to persuade her stiff legs to climb down, she saw something moving near the water.

"Hey," the person shouted when Bessie aimed her torch in that direction.

"Sorry," she said quickly, turning the light so that it showed the new arrival a path towards the rock.

"I didn't think you'd be here in the rain," a muffled voice said from inside the hooded coat.

"I was just about to give up on you," Bessie replied.

"Everyone else has," was the quiet reply.

"I'm Bessie."

"I'm Pat."

Bessie frowned. She couldn't tell if the person was male or female, and the name didn't help in the slightest. "It's nice to meet you, Pat," she said. "I assume you've been letting yourself into the last cottage to get out of the weather."

"It's cold and wet here."

"It is at that, especially in the winter, although often summer isn't much better."

Pat laughed, a sharp sound that was cut off as quickly as it had begun. "I should get the next boat back."

"Do you need money to buy a ticket?"

"You wanna pay for me to leave?"

"I want to help you. In my experience, no one chooses to sleep in an empty cottage if there are other options."

"That's where you're wrong. I choose to sleep there, even though I could let myself into any cottage on the beach. I could let myself into any house on the island. I've been thinking about spending a night or two in that big house on the cliff, actually. No one seems to be staying there at the moment."

"The family that lives there is away, but they have very good security."

"I could find a way in."

"Maybe you could. So why sleep in an empty cottage? Surely you'd prefer a bed."

"I thought no one would notice or care if I stayed in the empty one," Pat told her. "The beach is all but deserted, anyway, aside from your cottage and the one next to it. I didn't think anyone would be around until spring, and I'll be long gone by spring."

Bessie nodded. "You don't like to stay in one place for long?" she said, making the statement a question.

Pat shrugged. "I don't stay where I'm not welcome, and I'm not welcome anywhere."

"Is it difficult, finding a job?"

Pat gave another sharp bark of laughter. "With a record, it's impossible. No one wants to hire someone who's done time."

"If I had your talent for getting through locked doors, I think I might be tempted to use it, too," Bessie admitted. "It must come in handy."

"If I wanted to, I could steal whatever I wanted. I'd been in care since I was ten and I learned fast. Locks, security systems, those things aren't any problem for me."

"So you could be living very well indeed. Why sleep in an empty cottage on the beach?"

"I'm trying to do the right thing." Pat looked at Bessie and laughed. "That sounds stupid, but it's true. I've lived with, I don't know, maybe a dozen different foster families over the years. Out of all of them, there were maybe one or two people who really seemed to care. And then there was Beatrice."

"Beatrice?" Bessie repeated when Pat fell silent.

"She was old, maybe even as old as you," Pat told her.

"I'm not old," Bessie snapped.

Pat grinned. "Okay, well, she was old and she didn't mind admitting it. She used to brag about it, actually. She was seventy-six when I went to stay with her. Technically, she was too old to still be fostering, but where I was, they were a little bit desperate."

"So you were stuck with Beatrice," Bessie suggested.

"So Beatrice was stuck with me," Pat countered. "She was, well, she was the best. She actually made me go to school and encouraged me to think about the future. I'd been in and out of trouble my whole life, well, since I'd been ten. She was the one who made me want to stop doing things that were, well, illegal."

Pat went quiet again, staring at the sea, presumably remembering the past. Bessie shifted on the rock. It was cold and wet, but she didn't dare invite Pat inside her cottage. There seemed little doubt that Andrew would scare Pat away.

"Are you going to tell me the rest of the story?" Bessie asked eventually. "How did you get from Beatrice's house to this beach?"

"She used to holiday on the Isle of Man when she was younger," Pat replied. "She told me stories about strolling along Douglas promenade and riding the horse trams. She made the island out to be the most wonderful place in the world."

"I'm rather fond of it."

Pat laughed again. "I only got to stay with her for three months, and then I got moved again. She was deemed too old to be allowed to foster and I got sent to live with, well, that doesn't really matter. After another year, I aged out anyway, and that was the end of that. I was out on the street with nothing. I never did get any qualifications and I can't exactly list my actual skills on a job application, can I?"

"So you came over here?"

"I thought the island might be different. I thought maybe I could get away with not mentioning my criminal record, for one thing. I came over on the ferry, and I asked everyone for work. I've been doing some casual labour, getting a few pounds to pay for food, at least, but I can't afford a flat, which makes it hard to apply for anything more steady. Places want you to have an address, you know?"

"Do you really want to work?" Bessie asked.

Pat blinked. "I really do, and I want to go back to school, too, get some qualifications of some sort so that I can get a good job and make Beatrice proud."

"Do you drink or take drugs?"

"I'll have an odd pint if I have some extra money, but I never have any extra money. I don't take drugs. I've seen too much of what they can do to people."

"Come back at the same time tomorrow," Bessie told him. "I'll see what I can do to help."

Pat stared at her for a minute and then shrugged. "Maybe."

Bessie opened her mouth to reply, but Pat walked away before she could speak. Sighing, Bessie got down off the rock and slowly walked back towards her cottage, her legs and back aching from sitting on the hard and cold stone for such a long time.

"I'll do some investigating," Andrew replied once she'd told him the entire story.

"Whatever you find, I'm still going to try to help," Bessie countered as she sipped her tea. The warmth was only slowly working its way through her.

"How?"

"I thought I'd start with Maggie and Thomas," Bessie replied. "They have cottages to get ready for spring and Thomas isn't well enough to do much of the work. Maybe Pat could do some painting in exchange for being allowed to stay in one of the cottages."

"Assuming Pat is trustworthy."

Bessie waved a hand. "The cottages have nothing of value in them. The furniture was inexpensive when it was new and it's several years old now. Pat has proven to be quite capable of getting into the cottages anyway. It would be better for everyone if he or she was doing so with permission."

"I suppose I can't argue with that. It worries me that Pat got in here, though."

Bessie looked around her snug kitchen. "It worries me, too, but not enough to make me want to ring the police and have Pat arrested."

"You'll talk to Maggie or Thomas tomorrow?"

"First thing in the morning, if I can find them at home."

Bessie could tell that Andrew was worried about leaving her alone, knowing that Pat could easily get into Treoghe Bwaane again, but Bessie finally persuaded him that they both needed sleep.

"Push a chair up to the door after I leave," he suggested. "It won't stop anyone from getting the door open, but it should make quite a lot of noise."

"And I'll sleep with my mobile right next to my pillow," Bessie promised. She always did, actually, simply because that was where she kept her second charging cable. Plugging it in to charge just before bed was part of her evening routine now.

Bessie watched as Andrew crossed to his cottage. He waved from his doorway and then went inside. As Bessie shut her door, she wondered if he would be putting a chair behind his door as well. Feeling slightly foolish, she slid one of her kitchen chairs up to the door and then checked that she'd locked it tightly. A second chair was put behind the back door before Bessie headed up to bed.

When she opened her eyes the next morning, it was three minutes to six. Not feeling in any rush, she took her time over her shower and breakfast. By the time she headed out for her walk, the sun was making its way up and struggling to warm the cold November air. Marching briskly, she walked past the cottages, stopping behind the last one.

It was dark, and Bessie couldn't see anything to suggest that Pat was inside. That didn't mean anything, of course. On balance, it seemed highly likely that Pat was fast asleep in one of the bedrooms. After a moment, Bessie continued on, past the stairs to Thie yn Traie and then a bit further. As the wind picked up, she decided to turn back. A cuppa and a good book would be her reward once she'd rung Maggie, she decided, although she was really hoping she'd get Thomas rather than Maggie.

She was only a few paces away from her front door when she heard her name being shouted down the beach.

"Bessie? Hello?" Maggie called.

Turning around, Bessie forced herself to smile brightly at the woman. "Good morning," she said. "I was just going to ring you."

"Really? I hope nothing is wrong?"

"But what brings you down to the beach this early in the morning?" Bessie asked.

"I sneaked away while Thomas was still in bed. We've

ever so much to do to get the cottages ready for the spring and he will insist on trying to help, even though he's not really capable of doing much of anything these days." She sighed. "I don't know what to do, really. Maybe we should sell the cottages and move somewhere that's warm all year around."

"I may know of someone who can help," Bessie told her. "But before I tell you about that, you have to promise not to get angry."

"Angry? Why would I get angry?"

Bessie sighed. "Someone has been staying in the last cottage."

"I know. Or rather, I'd assumed as much. You were the one who spotted that the sliding door was ajar the other day, but there have been lots of other odd things going on there."

"There have?"

"For one thing, that cottage has never been so neat and tidy," Maggie replied. "Whoever is staying there is cleaning the cottage every day. I thought about leaving the person a note and asking him or her to simply move along the row and clean them all."

"I did leave the person a note," Bessie admitted. "And I spoke to Pat last night."

"Pat?"

"I didn't ask for a surname."

"And what did Pat have to say?"

"He or she spent years in foster care and then ended up on the street. One foster parent told Pat all about the Isle of Man, where she had holidayed years ago. Pat decided to come across and see about finding work, but hasn't had much luck."

"He or she? You aren't certain which?"

"I'm not. It was dark and it didn't seem to matter."

"So Pat came here and can't find work, so has been sleeping in my cottage."

"He or she has the talents necessary to break into any of the cottages. You should be grateful Pat is staying in the empty one."

"No doubt Pat is unaware that people were murdered in there," Maggie muttered.

"Regardless, you said yourself that the cottage is being kept clean. Why not offer Pat a job? You're going to have to hire someone to help with the cottages if you're going to have them ready for spring anyway. Why not hire Pat to help with the painting and the cleaning? Letting Pat stay in one of the cottages for the next few months would also give you a live-in security guard down here."

Maggie opened her mouth and then shut it again. "I'll have to discuss all of this with Thomas," she said eventually. "This person has been breaking into our cottage. What makes you think we can trust him, er, Pat?"

"As I said, Pat can easily break into anywhere and hasn't stolen anything yet."

"I'll talk to Thomas," Maggie replied. "I'll ring you later."

Bessie nodded. "I'm going to talk to Pat again tonight at ten."

Maggie frowned and then walked away, muttering something under her breath about breaking and entering and trustworthiness. Bessie sighed and walked the rest of the way back to her cottage. She'd done all she could for Pat for the moment. If Maggie said no, Bessie had some other options, but those could wait for another day.

Andrew was at her door just a few minutes later. "I saw you talking to Maggie when I opened my curtains, so I dawdled a bit," he told her with a wink.

"No doubt Maggie would have welcomed your opinion on what to do about Pat," Bessie replied.

"I wish I had an answer for her. I admire your desire to help, but the policeman in me worries about anyone trusting a complete stranger. I rang a few people to see if I could learn anything, but I'm afraid we simply don't have enough information to track Pat's history successfully."

"I may learn more tonight," Bessie replied, thinking that she also might decide not to share any additional information with Andrew. She wasn't terribly interested in Pat's past. Helping Pat going forward was her goal.

"And you're having lunch with a friend today, didn't you say?"

"I did."

"Do you have plans for this morning?"

Bessie shook her head.

"Shall we do something interesting, then?"

Bessie laughed. "Yes, let's. What did you have in mind?"

"I collected a pile of brochures from Castle Rushen when we were there, and I found one for the Gibbs of the Grove museum. I've never been there."

"It's a wonderful museum," Bessie told him. "And just the right size to fill a morning."

After the museum visit, Andrew kindly dropped Bessie off at the café in Lonan where she was meant to be meeting with Andy.

"Hello, Bessie," Jasmina, the café's owner, called as Bessie walked into the small building. "Sit anywhere." Jasmina was a friendly woman in her forties who had moved to the island after meeting a man online. The relationship hadn't worked out, but Jasmina was still here, happy to own the small café that was considerably larger than her previous location near the Laxey Wheel.

As Bessie looked around the room, she frowned at the number of empty tables. Jasmina was an excellent cook and a lovely person. Bessie had been hoping that the café would be a big success for her. It seemed likely that business was suffering because so many people had loved the restaurant that had been there before Jasmina had taken over, though.

"It's very quiet in here today," Bessie commented as Jasmina handed her a menu.

"We're usually quiet at midday," Jasmina replied.

"I'm sorry to hear that."

Jasmina laughed. "I'm not at all sorry. It's standing room only in here at breakfast time. I'm not certain why, but my breakfast menu is a huge success. Lunch is quieter, and I'm seriously considering not even being open in the evening. I'm making enough profit from breakfast alone to keep the place up and running, anyway."

"That's good to hear."

"What can I get for you?"

"I'm meeting a friend, so I'll just have a cup of tea for now," Bessie replied. She glanced at the menu and her stomach growled. Flushing, she looked up at Jasmina. "I hope my friend isn't too late."

Three additional customers came in before Andy finally strolled in at quarter past twelve. He nodded at Bessie and then crossed the room and sat down opposite her at the small table. His brown hair flopped over his eyes, and Bessie thought he looked not much older than the teens at the next table, even though she knew he'd left his teens behind years earlier.

"Hey," he said, picking up the menu.

Bessie waited until Jasmina had come back and taken their order before she spoke. As Andy sat back in his chair, she frowned at him. "Even at your worst, you were never actually rude," she said in a level tone.

He looked surprised and then sighed. "I'm sorry I'm late."

"Are you also sorry that you waited so long to return my call?" she asked.

He flushed and then nodded. "I've been busy."

"So I hear. How was Paris?"

Andy looked surprised and then shrugged. "It was nice, although I didn't get to see very much of the city. The course took up most of my time."

"And what did you learn?"

"It was all about puddings," Andy told her.

For the next several minutes, he talked about pastry and spun sugar and crème caramel, leaving Bessie nearly drooling in her seat. The passion in his eyes as he spoke reassured Bessie, at least.

"Here we are," Jasmina interrupted. She put their plates on the table. "Do you need anything else?"

"We're good," Andy told her.

Bessie took a bite of her beef stew, studying Andy as she chewed.

"Mum told me what you told her about Jennifer and the Seaview. She tells a very different story," he said after a moment.

"I'm sure she does, and I know whom I believe," Bessie replied.

Andy sighed. "You've never even met Jennifer."

"And I've known Jasper for many years. He wouldn't lie to me about such things. Jennifer booked several events at the Seaview and then cancelled them at the last minute. From what your mother said when I spoke to her last month, Jennifer managed to persuade you to cater those same events."

"Because the Seaview cancelled on her at the last minute, not the other way around," Andy said firmly. "They've been having trouble with their chef. I'm not surprised that Jasper doesn't want anyone to hear about that, though."

Bessie shook her head. "That Jasper and his head chef don't get along is common knowledge."

"As I understand it, you have friends who are staying at the Seaview fairly regularly and also using its conference facilities. No doubt Jasper wants to do everything in his power to convince you that everything is running smoothly there, regardless of the truth."

"I'm sorry, but I simply don't trust this Jennifer Johnson," Bessie told him.

Andy sighed. "That's a shame, because I've asked her to marry me."

CHAPTER 13

*B*essie stared at him for a minute. "You've done what?"

"I've asked her to marry me," he replied. "She's said yes, as well, I should add. We haven't set a date yet or anything, as there's no rush, but there's also no need to wait."

"Except you barely know one another," Bessie suggested.

"We've known each other for a few months. Lots of people get married more quickly than that."

"What about Elizabeth?" Bessie asked.

Andy made a face. "We had some fun together, but that's all it was, just fun."

"I thought you were good for one another."

"So did I, for a while, but she was impossible to understand. One day she'd be talking about getting married and having a family and the next day she'd decide that we were getting too serious and that maybe we should see other people. We were talking about buying a house together, you know that. Then she decided to go on an extended holiday with her parents."

"Her mother needed her to go along."

"Maybe, or maybe she simply wanted a long holiday. Whatever, she's been gone for more than six months. She can't possibly believe that I've waited for her, and I'm quite certain she's had a number of relationships while she's been gone."

"You haven't kept in touch?"

"I get the odd text message, but she's busy having a wonderful time and I'm busy working."

"Catering events for Jennifer."

"Yes, exactly. It pays well, and you know I love to cook."

"I thought you wanted to open your own restaurant."

"I do, one day," he said, staring down at his empty plate.

"Why not now?"

"I've been looking for the right location since I finished culinary school. It's not as easy as buying any old building and setting up shop, though. I want something special and I want it done to my standards."

"And you'll spend the next forty years chasing that dream and never actually accomplish anything," Bessie concluded.

Andy flushed. "I'm still looking," he told her.

"Why bother? It isn't as if you need the money. You may as well enjoy a life of leisure and stop worrying about having a restaurant."

"Having my own restaurant has been my dream since I was a child."

"Be careful what you wish for," Bessie told him. "For years it seemed an impossible dream and, now that you've the means to make it a reality, you're too afraid of failure to actually do anything."

"I don't have to be afraid of failure. I can afford to fail. According to my advocate, I can afford to fail multiple times," he said with a chuckle.

The laugh sounded hollow to Bessie. "Maybe you can

afford to fail financially, but I don't think your ego would survive."

He looked shocked and then put down his fork. "I think I've had quite enough of his conversation."

"Andy, I've known you since you were a child. You were a bright young man who struggled because of difficult circumstances. Now you're an intelligent adult who seems to be struggling with what some would see as ideal circumstances."

"Money doesn't solve all of life's problems," he muttered.

"No, it doesn't. And it doesn't automatically bring happiness, either. You still have to find the things that bring you joy. Money also brings different problems, such as difficulty in determining which of your friends are true friends."

"Jennifer isn't after my money," he said flatly. "She even suggested that we donate most of it to charity and simply live off what we can earn ourselves."

"Are you considering the idea?"

He shrugged. "Right now I'm just focussed on helping her build her business. Elizabeth will be back soon and I want Jennifer to be ready for the competition."

"There is another party planner on the island now, too, isn't there?"

Andy grinned. "Yeah, but Jake isn't competition for anyone — not really, anyway. He's doing his best, but he's not had a lot of success. I believe he's going back to his old job soon."

"Which was what?"

"He was an electrician and he made good money, but then he helped a friend plan his wedding and he really enjoyed doing so. What he didn't seem to realise is that his friend did at least half of the work, and that friend isn't interested in planning parties for a living. Anyway, the real competition will be between Elizabeth and Jennifer."

"And you'll be caught at the centre."

"Not at all. I'm supporting Jennifer completely. One of the things she'll be planning soon will be our wedding, of course."

Bessie sighed. "Whatever happened in your personal relationship, I'm certain Elizabeth will be sorry to have lost you as her favourite caterer for special events."

"She's going to have to work a lot harder to get customers now," Andy said, sounding smugly satisfied by that fact.

"And Jennifer will have people beating down her door to get you to cater their events."

Andy shrugged. "I'm really helping out only in emergencies. I truly am looking for a restaurant location. I want to find a house now, too, especially since I'm getting married. I'm doing one event this week, and that's only because a cafe in Onchan cancelled on her at the last minute."

"Did they, now?" Bessie asked, instantly suspicious.

"They did," Andy said firmly. "She wouldn't lie to me."

"Which café in Onchan?"

He opened his mouth and then snapped it shut again. "I'm not going to tell you," he said after a moment. "You'll only go and ask them about it. I wouldn't be at all surprised if they lied to you, anyway, to hide how unreliable they are."

Bessie sighed. "I worry about my friends," she said softly. "I don't want to see you get hurt."

"Jennifer and I are going to be very happy together," he told her. "And she's going to be a big success, whether I'm catering for her or not."

"And you're going to get your restaurant open before the end of next year?"

"Maybe."

Bessie put her hand on his and then waited until he looked at her to speak again. "Promise me that you'll have your restaurant open before the end of next year," she said.

"I don't want to rush things."

"I know, but that gives you thirteen months. That doesn't seem at all rushed."

"I haven't even found the right location yet."

"So settle for a less than right location. Jasmina is doing well here, and this place isn't convenient for anyone. Dan and Carol Jenkins did extremely well here, too."

He shrugged. "We'll see."

"I was going to ask you to cater Thanksgiving for me later this month," Bessie said after a moment.

"I could, if you have Jennifer do the planning for you."

Bessie shook her head. "I've been having Thanksgiving celebrations on the island since well before you were born. I don't need anyone else to help me with this year's event. Even if you can't cater it, you'll be invited, of course. You and Jennifer."

"We'll have to see what else we're doing that day," he replied.

"Promise me that you'll come and see me once in a while," she said, hoping for at least that much.

"I'll try, but, as I said, I'm quite busy."

"Too busy for your old friends."

"It isn't that at all," Andy replied. "I'll come and visit once in a while."

"Good, I'll expect you on the first of the month," Bessie told him.

He looked surprised and then laughed. "I can manage that. Christmas will still be a long way off by then."

"You won't be getting married until the new year, I hope."

"I don't think so. Jennifer isn't certain whether she wants a big, fancy wedding or if she wants to run away somewhere. We've discussed both options but haven't made any decision yet."

"I want to meet her, and soon. Bring her on the first."

"You don't trust her."

"I don't know her and I worry about you."

"I'm a good judge of character."

Or so you believe, Bessie thought. "Indulge me," she requested.

He nodded and then sighed. "I'm sorry. I'm not really myself at the moment," he said in a low voice. "I thought I would come back from school and find the perfect house and restaurant and live happily ever after. It isn't working out that way at all."

"Pudding?" Jasmina asked. She glanced at Andy and blushed. "I shouldn't even offer you pudding. I know you're an expert."

Andy shook his head. "I'm not an expert, I'm just a man who loves puddings. I'll have the sticky toffee pudding, please."

Jasmina nodded. "Bessie?"

"Me too," she replied. "How is your mother?" she asked Andy as Jasmina walked away.

The pair chatted about Anne and about other neutral topics as they enjoyed their puddings. As Jasmina was collecting their pudding plates, Bessie had a thought.

"Jasmina, do you have time for a chat later?" she asked.

The woman looked surprised but then shrugged. "When?"

"What time do you close tonight?"

"Probably around seven. I usually get a few customers between five and six, but they're almost always gone by seven."

"I'll come back before seven, then," Bessie said.

"See you later, then," Jasmina replied, looking curious, but not asking any questions.

"I'll come and see you on the first," Andy promised as he walked with Bessie out of the building. "How are you getting home?"

"I'll ring for a taxi."

"I can take you."

Bessie thought about protesting, but decided she'd rather have more time to talk with Andy. "Tell me more about Jennifer," she suggested as he started his car.

"She's from Liverpool, but she moved to the island just over a year ago to work for one of the banks. She's always enjoyed planning parties. She used to do it for all of her friends, and one of them finally persuaded her to start charging for her services. Within a few months, she was so busy that she had to quit her job at the bank so she could do party planning full-time."

"Is her family all in Liverpool, then?"

"Her parents are there. She has a sister in Brighton and a brother in New Zealand."

"Interesting."

"Apparently, her parents are considering moving, but they aren't certain where they want to go. Her mother wants to be closer to one of the children, but obviously there is a big difference between Brighton and New Zealand. From what Jennifer said, they aren't really considering the Isle of Man, although I don't know why."

"You haven't met them yet?"

"I haven't had a chance. They've only been to the island once in the time that Jennifer has been here, and she doesn't go back to Liverpool very often. We were talking about going across to see them one day, but, obviously, it's very difficult for Jennifer to get away. She's a victim of her own success, really. When she worked at the bank, she had weekends off, but now she's busier on weekends than during the week."

Bessie nodded. "And what does your mother think of Jennifer?"

"They're cordial to one another," Andy replied.

Cordial? Interesting, Bessie thought.

Andy drove down the hill to Bessie's cottage. As the cottage came into view, he sighed. "I wish I could bottle up the way I feel when I see your cottage."

"How do you feel?"

"As if I've come back to the one place that's truly safe and welcoming," he said softly. "I shouldn't say that, as Mum's cottage is both of those things now that she's on her own, but there are a lot of bad memories there, too. I keep urging her to move, but she claims to have too many good memories there."

"It's been her home since she was born."

"Yes, and it was mine for my entire life, too. I couldn't wait to leave, but I don't have to tell you that."

"Come in for a cuppa," Bessie suggested.

"I'd like that," Andy replied, a huge grin spreading over his face.

He was climbing out of the car when his mobile rang. The expression on his face when he looked at the device wasn't a happy one. "Hello?"

"I told you I was having lunch with a friend."

"I'll be another hour or so."

"Because I will."

"Can't it wait?"

He glanced at his watch and sighed. "I'll be there in ten minutes," he said.

Bessie raised an eyebrow.

Andy dropped his phone back into his pocket. "I'm awfully sorry," he said. "Jennifer is having car trouble and she needs to get to an appointment."

"Would you like the number of my taxi firm?"

Andy laughed. "I'd love to send her a taxi, but she'd be very upset if I did. I need to go."

A dozen different replies sprang to Bessie's lips, but she swallowed them all. "I'm sorry to hear that," was what she finally said.

"I will come and visit soon."

"You're welcome any time, but I'm expecting you on the first," she reminded him.

"I'll be here, with or without Jennifer."

"I hope it's with. I'd quite like to meet her."

Andy pulled her into a tight hug. "Thank you," he whispered in her ear.

"I haven't done anything."

"You care, and for a great many years, I often felt as if you were the only one who did. I'll always be grateful to you."

He walked Bessie to her door and made sure she was safely inside before he sprinted back to his car and drove away. Bessie pushed the door shut with sigh. Andy clearly had a lot on his mind, and Jennifer seemed to be his biggest problem. *Why in the world had he asked her to marry him?*

Still worried about Andy, Bessie tried to settle down with a book, but couldn't find one that would keep her interest. After half an hour, having discarded more than a dozen titles, Bessie gave up and put on her shoes. It was cold, but dry, and she hoped a long walk would clear her head.

Although she tried to avoid it, Bessie found herself staring at the last cottage as she walked past it. It looked as deserted at it usually did, but Bessie couldn't help but wonder if Pat was inside. When she reached the stairs to Thie yn Traie, she turned around. She'd taken just a few steps when she heard someone calling her name.

"Aunt Bessie?"

The sound seemed to be coming from above her, and Bessie felt oddly unsettled as she looked around, trying to work out from where it had come.

"I'm up here," the voice called.

Bessie looked up at the cliff face and then smiled as she spotted Jack Hooper making his way down the steep staircases that ran from Thie yn Traie to the beach. It was more of a collection of short sets of stairs that were only tenuously linked than a proper stairway to the beach, and Bessie found herself holding her breath as the man made a slow descent.

"Hello," he said as he stepped off the last step.

"Hello," she replied before being pulled into a hug.

Jack had grown up in Laxey, and Bessie remembered him as a ginger-haired little boy who'd managed to fall into the sea with alarming regularity. He and his family had left the island some years earlier, and while they'd been in the UK, he'd trained as a butler. Bessie had been thrilled when George and Mary Quayle had hired him to work at Thie yn Traie. He'd been with them on their long holiday, and Bessie was delighted to see him again.

"How are you?" she asked when he released her.

"I'm well, thank you. It's been an interesting seven months since I was last here. I've been all over the world. It's been amazing and I've loved every minute of it, but I'm awfully glad to be home again."

"How are George and Mary?"

"They're well. Mr. Quayle is the same as ever, really. I do hope he'll be welcomed back to the island, in spite of all of the unpleasantness with Grant Robertson. Mr. Quayle has missed his active social life. Mrs. Quayle has had a few minor health issues, mostly brought on by stress, I believe, but she's been much better this past month. They're both looking forward to coming home, though."

"And Elizabeth?"

"Is, well, Miss Elizabeth," he laughed. "She wanted to do everything and see everything everywhere that we went, but she complained a great deal about missing the island, as well."

Bessie sighed. "She should know that two new party planning businesses have opened since she's been gone."

Jack nodded. "My mother has kept me informed, and Miss Elizabeth is aware that she'll have competition when she gets back."

"And are you also aware that Andy has been working extensively with one of them?" Bessie asked.

"Yes, apparently Miss Jennifer Johnson has been keeping Andy so busy that he hasn't had time to find either a location for his restaurant or a house to purchase."

"I had lunch with Andy. He's asked Jennifer to marry him," Bessie blurted out.

Jack frowned. "I'm not certain I want to share that information with Miss Elizabeth," he said.

"I don't blame you."

"She did go out once in a while with other men while we were travelling, but it was never anything serious. I was under the impression that she is in love with Mr. Caine."

"Whether she is or not, he seems to be quite taken by Jennifer Johnson."

"What do you think of her?"

"I've not met her. I was wondering if I should plan a party, though."

Jack chuckled. "Miss Elizabeth would never forgive you if you let that woman plan a party for you."

"I've little choice with Elizabeth away."

"The family will be back on the island before the end of the month. It will probably take them a few days to get settled before they'll be ready for guests, though."

"I'm looking forward to seeing Mary again."

"She's missed you. I believe she sent you a few postcards."

Bessie nodded. "Several, from exotic locations I'll never visit."

"I never thought I'd visit them, either. You never know where life will take you."

"That's very true," Bessie agreed, thinking about the cold case unit that had given her her very first pay cheque.

The pair chatted for a while longer before Jack glanced at his watch. "I need to get back to work," he exclaimed. "There's a great deal that needs to be done to get the house ready for the family."

Bessie gave him another hug and then watched as he climbed back up the stairs. It wasn't until he was safely at the top that she continued on her way.

When she reached Andrew's cottage, she knocked on his door.

"Good afternoon," he said. "I was wondering if you were back from your lunch yet."

"I am, but I'm meeting with someone later. I thought you might like to come along."

"Pat?"

"No, although I am doing that as well, but not until ten. No, this meeting is at seven in Lonan. I'm sure you remember Jasmina, who used to run the little restaurant near the Laxey Wheel. She moved to the island after meeting a man on the Internet. I want to try to better understand how that sort of relationship develops."

Andrew grinned at her. "I'm intrigued already."

CHAPTER 14

They walked to Bessie's cottage, where her answering machine light was flashing. She sighed and then pressed the button to play her messages.

"Thomas and I want to meet Pat. We'll be at your cottage at ten." Maggie's voice seemed to fill the kitchen.

"I hope that's good news," Andrew said.

"I was expecting it. I just don't know if they want to meet Pat to offer a job or threaten to ring the police. I suppose I'll find out tonight."

"I'll be here as well, just in case."

Bessie frowned. "Would you be terribly offended if I asked you to stay in the sitting room while Pat is here? I'm afraid Pat will be overwhelmed enough by Thomas and Maggie."

"I'll hide in the sitting room, but I will interrupt if I feel it's necessary."

They talked together about nothing much until Bessie's stomach began to rumble. "Where can we go for dinner?" Andrew asked.

"Well, Jasmina does own a café. I had lunch there, but the food is good and she said she isn't too busy in the evening."

"If you don't mind eating there again, it will simplify our evening."

Just before six, they headed to Lonan. Jasmina laughed as they walked into the café.

"You really are eager to talk to me, aren't you?" she asked Bessie.

"We thought we might have dinner here before our chat," Bessie explained.

"Sit anywhere," Jasmina replied, waving an arm.

There was a couple sitting together in one corner, but otherwise the café was empty. Andrew led Bessie to a table as far from the others as possible.

Jasmina took their order and then delivered food to the other table. Bessie and Andrew were still eating when the other couple left.

"I'll just turn the sign around," Jasmina said. She flipped the sign on the door from "Open" to "Closed" and turned off most of the exterior lights. Then she crossed the room and sat down next to Bessie.

"I hope there isn't anything wrong," she said, looking nervous.

"Not at all," Bessie assured her. "I was reading an article about a man who'd met a woman on the Internet. He'd flown halfway around the world to meet her in person, and she turned out to be not at all the way she'd described herself."

Jasmina nodded. "You'd be surprised how many people lie about themselves, although I think some people have an overinflated idea of their own appeal, as well."

"I remembered you once telling me that you'd met Richard Stern online. He was the reason you moved to the island, wasn't he?" Bessie asked.

Jasmina flushed. "That's a bottle of wine kind of question," she said softly.

"I don't want to pry," Bessie said quickly. "I'm simply trying to understand how such relationships develop. I'm sure it's different for every couple, as well, but I was hoping you could share some general information, that's all."

"It's fine, really. Trusting Richard wasn't one of my smarter decisions, but it's all worked out in the end. I'd never even considered moving to the Isle of Man before I met him, and now I can't imagine living anywhere else."

"It's a lovely island," Andrew said. "I keep finding excuses to come back. If circumstances were different, I would be very tempted to move here myself."

"What do you want to know?" Jasmina asked.

"How did you first meet Richard?" was Bessie's first question.

"There are online matchmaking agencies, but I've never tried them. We actually met in a chat room."

Bessie looked at Andrew, who shrugged.

"What's a chat room?" Bessie asked.

"It's a place you can go to, well, chat to people around the world. Richard and I met in one that was for people who enjoy *Strangers*."

"Strangers?" Bessie echoed.

"It's an American situation comedy," Andrew told her. "It's hugely popular both there and here."

"And there's a chat room about it," Bessie said.

"There are several, actually," Jasmina told her. "I belong to several and usually chat in them most days. Back in the UK, I worked in a shop, behind the till. I was allowed to use the shop's computer for chatting when it wasn't busy, which was most of the time."

"And Richard was also a member of the same chat group?" Bessie asked.

"He was. He made some comment about one of the actresses looking a bit heavier these days, and I replied that I'd heard she was pregnant but that they weren't writing her pregnancy into the show. We talked back and forth for a day or two and then he sent me a private chat. We carried on talking, just the two of us, for ages."

Bessie nodded. "About the television show?"

"At first, and then about other things. We talked for about a week, maybe a bit longer, before things started to get more personal. I told him about Tamazin at that point, and about my divorce."

"Tamazin?" Andrew asked.

"My daughter. She's a teenager and the light of my life."

Andrew smiled. "So what happened next?"

"After about a month, during which we'd talked about a million different things, he asked me for my telephone number. The first time we talked on the phone it all felt just right. He sounded smart and funny and he said all the right things. I'd told him that I'd always wanted to have my own restaurant and he said he could help me with that. It was stupid to believe him, of course, but by that time I felt as if I knew him."

"So you moved to the island," Bessie said.

"Oh, not right away. We talked on the phone every night for over a month, and then Richard came to visit me. He stayed with me, sleeping on the couch, I should add, for a week. It was only after that visit that I decided to move to the island."

"Would you have come to visit him if he hadn't gone to you?" Bessie asked.

"I don't know. He was between jobs, so it was easier for him to travel. Besides, I had Tamazin to worry about. I couldn't leave her alone for a week and I wasn't about to let her stay with her father. I didn't really have anyone else to leave her with, and I'm not sure I'd have wanted to bring her with me, under the circumstances."

"So how long were you talking before you actually met in person?" Bessie wondered.

"Four and a half months, maybe," Jasmina replied, frowning and looking up at the ceiling as she spoke. "Maybe five months, certainly not less than four."

Bessie looked at Andrew.

"Do you know of other people who've met potential partners online?" he asked Jasmina.

"I have quite a few friends who've tried online matchmaking services," she told him. "So far, none of them have found their next husband that way."

"If Richard had lived in America or New Zealand or somewhere else considerably further away, would you have done things differently?"

"I doubt I would have bothered chatting with him at all, once I'd discovered where he lived. I mean, I'd have talked with him about the television show, but I wouldn't have bothered getting more personal. Relationships over great distances and involving different countries are a good deal more complicated."

Bessie nodded. "And now, I'd quite fancy a slice of your chocolate cake," she told Jasmina.

"There's chocolate cake?" Andrew asked.

Jasmina laughed and got to her feet. "Two slices of cake, then. I won't be long."

"Of course, all of that proves nothing," Andrew said as Jasmina walked away.

"I know, but I found it interesting anyway. What she said made me think it even less likely that Paul flew all that way to meet a woman he knew only from a handful of emails."

"It's possible there were more emails, but that the experts were unable to recover them from the laptop."

"There aren't any obvious gaps in the existing ones, though, and the last few talk about his upcoming visit to New York. I don't suppose it's possible that he'd visited New York previously?"

"Jeff did check. While Paul did travel occasionally, that trip was his first to New York."

Jasmina sat and chatted with them about nothing much as they ate their puddings. The cake was every bit as delicious as Bessie had been expecting.

"Thank you for everything," she told Jasmina as she and Andrew got ready to leave.

"Thanks for coming. I don't know that I've had a customer visit me twice in one day before," Jasmina told her.

They were back at Bessie's cottage a short while later.

"I'll just go and check my emails while we wait for ten o'clock," Andrew told Bessie at her door.

"Don't be too long. I'll put the kettle on," she replied.

He knocked just after the kettle had boiled. Bessie made tea and got down some of her favourite chocolate biscuits. When she sat down opposite the man, she noticed that he was smiling broadly.

"You've learned something," she guessed.

"It isn't much, but it's something," he agreed. "Jeff had a chance to speak to Max today, or maybe it was yesterday. Anyway, he's spoken to Max."

"And what did he learn from Max?"

"At the moment, Max is in Berlin, still working for the same company, but he's considering another secondment, this time to Paris."

"Good for him. What did he say about Paul?" Bessie demanded.

Andrew chuckled. "Sorry, I shouldn't tease. Jeff asked him again about Prisoners of Cardavar. He'd admitted, back when Paul died, that he'd tried the game a few times, but apparently he was downplaying just how much he actually does play the game. He's admitted now that he plays nearly every day and that he'd joined several gaming groups in New York while he was there. He still insists that he'd been unaware of the Internet newsgroup at the time of Paul's death, but he did admit that he belongs to it now."

"Is there any way to find out exactly when he joined?" Bessie asked.

"Jeff is trying to get that information, but there are ways to do things online anonymously, as well. Jeff also asked him for more information about Paul, though."

Andrew stopped to take a sip of tea. Bessie took a huge bite of biscuit to keep herself from speaking. The man was teasing again, and she wasn't going to give him the satisfaction of demanding that he continue.

"According to Max, Paul didn't cheat, not on Anja or on any other woman with whom he'd been involved. Obviously, he hadn't seen Paul in six months or more, but he said that he'd known Paul reasonably well and that he couldn't imagine him sneaking away to see another woman behind Anja's back."

"Interesting."

"In light of that, Jeff asked him what he could see Paul sneaking away to America to do. Max said that Paul would have done something like that to help a friend."

"Even more interesting. Jeff needs to find Leon."

Andrew nodded. "That's definitely his next priority. He still wants to find Maria, or the person or persons who pretended to be Maria, but I believe he's starting to think that the solution to the case may lie elsewhere."

A knock on the door kept Bessie from replying. She opened the door to Maggie and Thomas. Maggie looked upset. Bessie thought Thomas looked slightly better than he had the last time she'd seen him, but that wasn't saying much.

The man had been fighting various illnesses for what felt like years now. He'd had pneumonia a number of times, and Bessie wasn't certain how many times he'd been hospitalised. He was gaunt and pale, but he gave Bessie a big smile and a quick hug.

"Let me make you some tea," Bessie offered.

"I'll be up all night if I drink anything now," Maggie told her. "You should know that I think this is a bad idea. I don't trust this Pat person and I don't want anyone in that last cottage."

"Which is just as well, as that cottage isn't habitable," Thomas said. "Pat can move into one of the other cottages, though. They're just sitting empty. My doctors want me to spend at least some of the winter months somewhere warmer. If Pat wants to act as security for the cottages while we're away in exchange for a place to stay, I think we'd all be better off."

"And do some painting," Maggie added.

Thomas nodded. "Of course, we'd pay for the time the painting takes."

Maggie made a face and then sat down at the table. "Where is Pat, then?" she demanded.

"I'll go and collect hi, er, Pat," Bessie said. "You can all wait here."

Maggie looked as if she wanted to object, but Bessie knew it was far too cold for Thomas to be standing around outside. She put on her shoes and her coat and headed for the back door.

"I'll be out of sight when you get back," Andrew assured her before she left.

She crossed to the rock and perched on top of it. It was cold, but at least it was dry. The waves lapped against the sand, getting closer to Bessie, but still far enough away for her feet to stay dry. The moon provided enough light for

Bessie to switch off her torch. After a few deep breaths, she felt herself relaxing. Sitting on the beach often brought back memories for Bessie, and tonight she found herself thinking about former friends who had passed away long ago.

"Hello."

The voice made Bessie jump. She turned and smiled at Pat. "I was a million miles away," she said. "Actually, I was about fifty years away, remembering an old friend."

"I never had much chance to make friends."

"You have me now."

Pat laughed. "I suppose."

"Maggie and Thomas Shimmin, the couple who own the cottages, are here. They'd like to speak to you about maybe having you stay in one of them to act as security for them," Bessie said.

"Security? Me? That's funny, since I'm the one doing the breaking and entering."

"But you aren't the only one. They've had other issues in the winter months. Come inside and talk to them, please. You don't have to agree, but at least you can hear what they have to say."

Pat took a step backwards. "I don't think so."

"You told me that you wanted to work. I believed you said you wanted to make Beatrice proud."

"I shouldn't have told you about Beatrice."

"It's up to you," Bessie said, getting down off the rock. "I was trying to help, but you have to want to change. If you aren't ready to do that, then I suggest you find a new place to stay. Eventually the police will catch you in that last cottage. When they do, they'll send you back to the UK."

Pat sighed. "I'll talk to them, but I don't know about working for them."

Inside the cottage, Bessie gave Pat a cup of tea and a few biscuits. In Bessie's kitchen, it was obvious that Pat needed a shave, which seemed to answer the question about his gender, anyway.

Bessie sat down at the table and then sat back and let Thomas do the talking. After half an hour, he'd persuaded Pat that staying in the cottages legally was better than breaking and entering.

"I don't know anything about painting," Pat warned Thomas when he suggested that he would pay to have that job done.

"If you're willing to learn, I can teach you what you need to know," Thomas replied. "We can talk more about it once you're settled in one of the cottages."

Pat simply shrugged.

After a few more biscuits, Thomas, Maggie, and Pat went to look over the cottages so that Pat could pick out a temporary home. After they left, Andrew emerged from the sitting room.

"I offered to investigate Pat's background, but Thomas doesn't want to know," he told Bessie. "He's prepared to give Pat a chance, regardless. I thought Maggie was going to explode, but he insisted."

"I just hope it all goes well. I'll feel terrible if Pat ends up stealing from the cottages or does some sort of serious damage to one of them or something."

"I may see what I can find, just out of curiosity," Andrew replied.

They were talking about their plans for the next day when someone knocked.

"I just wanted to let you know that Pat will be staying in number four," Maggie told them. "He's moved his things into the cottage, but he doesn't have much. I've told him I may bring down a few bags of clothes, things that were Thomas's before he lost so much weight. There may be one or two things that Pat could use. I'd appreciate it if you could keep an eye on him," she said, directing the last sentence towards Andrew.

"I will," he assured her.

As Andrew was hoping for another email from Jeff, they agreed that he'd spend the morning at home. "I'll collect you at half one for the meeting," he told Bessie when she let him out. "I can't help but feel as if we're getting close to a break-through."

Bessie nodded. "I feel the same way, but I've been wrong about such things before."

As she locked the door behind the man, she started questioning her words, though. Had she ever been wrong when she'd thought they were getting near to solving a case? With that question on her mind, she went up and took herself to bed.

* * *

HEAVY RAIN MEANT she had to change her plans for the next morning. She'd been hoping to take a long walk, maybe to visit Grace and Aalish, but there was no way she was going to slog through wind, rain, and wet sand that far. Instead, she put on her raincoat and her Wellington boots and walked as quickly as she could to Thie yn Traie. As she walked back past the cottages, she spotted Pat standing in the sitting room of cottage four. She waved, but didn't stop.

Lunch was a bowl of soup and some toast. No doubt there would be something wonderful to eat at the Seaview, and she wanted to save room. Besides, Andrew had suggested that they go out for a nice meal that evening. A large lunch might spoil her appetite for later.

When she opened the door to Andrew's knock at half one, he had another huge smile on his face.

"You've learned something," she said.

He nodded. "And I can't tell you anything until we're all together, so let's go."

Bessie laughed. "Even if we rush, the others won't be there yet," she reminded him as she slipped on her shoes. Even though that was true, she found herself hurrying to pull on her coat and lock the door to the cottage. They were in the car before she spoke again.

"Have we solved the case, then?" she asked.

"Unfortunately, not yet, but Jeff has a new area to investigate and things are looking promising."

Of course, Bessie had dozens more questions that she wanted to ask, but she knew Andrew wouldn't want to tell her anything until the group was together. She stared out the window, thinking about all of the possibilities. *Has Jeff found Maria? Has someone from the building site revealed something new? Or has Jeff tracked down Leon?* Hoping it was the last of those, Bessie took a few deep breaths and sat back in her seat. Ramsey suddenly seemed a good deal further away than usual.

CHAPTER 15

*J*asper was waiting to show them to a conference room on the first floor. "I caught Dan Ross snooping around the grounds this morning," he told them as they boarded the lift. "When I threatened to ring the police, he told me he'd come for breakfast. I walked him to the restaurant and took his order myself."

Bessie laughed. "I hope he felt that he had to order a large breakfast."

"I'm rather hoping he comes back this afternoon," Jasper replied. "We don't serve afternoon tea every day, but I'll make an exception for him."

The conference room was very similar to the one they normally used. The catering staff was busy in the back of the room setting out the food and drinks.

"Tea, coffee, and a pot of drinking chocolate today," Jasper said. "I thought it might sound good on such a cold afternoon."

"It does sound good," Bessie said, heading for the table.

"Give it a good stir before you pour yourself a cup," the waiter moving plates told her.

Bessie did as she was told and then took her cup of hot chocolate to the table. She'd go back for food once the staff was finished, she'd decided.

Andrew took a seat and began to flip through the folder he'd pulled out of his briefcase. With nothing else to do, Bessie began to look back through the case file, even though she felt as if she'd memorized it already. The door swung open a few minutes later.

"What a miserable day," Doona muttered as she and John walked into the room.

"Good afternoon," John said. He looked at Andrew and smiled. "There's been a break in the case, hasn't there?"

Andrew chuckled. "I never realised how transparent my facial expressions are. Bessie guessed the same thing when she saw me."

"You've a gleam in your eyes," John said. "As if you've something exciting to tell everyone."

Before Andrew could reply, Hugh walked into the room, carrying a large backpack. He nodded at Bessie and then looked at Andrew. "Good news?" he asked. He looked confused as everyone else burst out laughing.

"What's in the bag?" Bessie asked after Andrew had explained the laughter to Hugh.

"Textbooks," he replied. "I got more done here the other day after our meeting than I can at home in twice as much time. Jasper offered me the use of a conference room whenever I want one, so I thought I'd do some homework after the meeting. I'm working a late shift tonight, and if I go home, I won't get anything done."

The catering staff had finished setting up, so everyone filled plates and then took their seats at the table. Doona was as happy to see the drinking chocolate as Bessie had been, and Hugh poured himself a cup of it as well.

"I've been drinking too much coffee lately," he explained. "This should be a nice change."

Harry walked in as Bessie was considering refilling her cup. "Andrew's excited about something," he commented. He glanced around the table and then looked at Bessie. "Shall I refill that for you?" he asked.

"Yes, please," she said, trying to hide her surprise.

When he returned to the table, he was carrying his own cup of coffee as well as Bessie's chocolate. He dropped into the seat next to hers as Charles walked into the room.

"I have to ring someone at half two," he said as a greeting before sitting down and pulling out his mobile. He set the phone on the table and then looked at Andrew. "Do we have much to discuss?" he asked.

"I have updates on just about everything," Andrew replied. "I'll save the most interesting of them for last."

Bessie picked up her cup and took a sip of chocolate. The smooth sweetness kept her from arguing with Andrew.

"Harry, I've read your report. It's all very interesting, but I'm not certain it's getting us any closer to finding Paul's killer," Andrew said.

Harry nodded. "I've been emailing back and forth with three different people, all of whom I suspect may be planning to try to extort money from me, but I don't believe any of them are linked to Maria."

"Are you planning to keep talking with them?" John asked.

"Oh, yes," Harry said. "I'm working with the technology department back in London now. They may take over eventually, but for now, I'm, well, enjoying might be the wrong word, but let's say enjoying the experience."

"Charles, your report was interesting as well," Andrew said.

Charles looked up from his phone. "My friend, Wayne,

has discovered four women named Maria who used to live in the building that he identified. He's been able to locate two of them and eliminate them from our enquiries. He's going to keep working to locate the other two unless we determine that his efforts are unnecessary."

"Jeff spent some time with the men who were fitting the carpets in the flat where the body was found," Andrew said. "Two of the men are Prisoners of Cardavar players."

"Did either of them know about the newsgroup?" Charles asked.

"No, but one of them remembered a woman named Maria who used to play at one of the bars he frequents."

"That sounds promising," John said.

"The man in question is going to talk to his gaming friends to see if any of them know anything about Maria. He thought it was possible that she went out with one of his acquaintances a few times. He's going to get back to Jeff with more information soon," Andrew said.

"So we have a solid lead on Maria," Hugh said.

"We have a solid lead on a Maria," Andrew replied. "At this point, we've nothing to tie the two Marias together. It's a fairly common name, after all, and New York City is a big place."

"So there's something else," Bessie said. "That isn't enough to put that gleam in your eyes."

Andrew laughed. "There is something else," he agreed. "I emailed you all with the information that Jeff got from Max. He's had a chance to speak to Leon now, as well."

"He's back in Berlin, didn't you say?" John asked.

"He is back in Berlin," Andrew agreed. "The relationship that he moved to America to pursue didn't work out and he moved back to Berlin not long after Paul's death, actually."

"So what did he have to say? Did he suddenly remember

that he knows Maria or something?" Charles asked impatiently.

"Jeff asked him about Paul and Leon told him that Paul was never faithful to any woman with whom he'd ever been involved," Andrew replied.

"Max said the opposite," Bessie said.

Andrew nodded. "Leon said that he wasn't at all surprised when he'd heard that Paul had sneaked away in order to meet another woman. According to him, Paul liked variety in his bedroom, regardless of his relationship status."

"Surely, if that were true, Anja would have known or at least suspected something," Bessie argued.

"And that brings us to the most interesting part," Andrew told her. "Leon is now engaged to Anja."

There were gasps all around the table. Bessie took a sip of chocolate while she thought about what Andrew had said. Hugh was the first to speak.

"He'd ended his relationship with her before she got involved with Paul. When his relationship in New York didn't work out, he must have decided he wanted her back," he guessed.

"Except by that time she was already engaged to Paul," Doona added.

"So he found a way to get Paul to come to New York and then he killed him," Hugh concluded.

Andrew held up a hand. "At this point, we're simply speculating, but one thing that's been missing throughout this investigation is a motive. No one seemed to have any reason to kill Paul. Now we may have found a possible motive for someone connected to the case. Jeff is going to focus his attention on Leon. We're both hopeful that he'll be able to find evidence to back up our suspicions."

"Max said that Paul would have flown to New York to help a friend in trouble," Bessie said thoughtfully.

"So where does Maria fit into all of this?" Harry demanded.

"Bessie noticed something on the emails when she first looked at them," Andrew told him. "They all have the same date and time stamp. Jeff explained that away by citing the amount of damage that the computer had sustained, but he's going to go back to his experts and get them to take a closer look. Leon works with computers, and Jeff believes it's possible that he wrote all of the emails and loaded them onto Paul's computer to make it appear as if Paul was in New York to meet a stranger. Then he damaged the computer to cover his tracks."

"So Maria might not have ever existed?" Doona asked.

"Possibly not," Andrew replied. "We're still a long way off from proving that, though. Jeff wants to get access to Leon's computers, but that's easier said than done."

"Does he have a good contact with the German police?" John asked.

"He does, and so do I," Andrew replied. "They're keeping a very close eye on Leon while the investigation continues."

"It appears that Bessie may have been right again," Harry said, giving Bessie an appraising look.

"She is brilliant," Hugh said. "Even the dice knew it."

Everyone laughed, and then Andrew continued.

"I don't think there's much more we can do for now," he said. "I'll be on the island for another week, although Harry and Charles have flights back to London tomorrow. I'll keep everyone informed if I hear anything else."

Harry nodded and got to his feet. "I'll see you all in December, then," he said as he headed for the door.

"I thought maybe we could all have dinner together tonight," Andrew said quickly.

Harry hesitated and then shrugged. "Why not?"

"We'll meet in the restaurant here at six," Andrew told him.

Harry nodded and then left the room. Charles was right behind him. "I'll be at dinner if I can get what I need to do done by six," he called over his shoulder as he dashed out of the room.

"They still don't seem very fond of the rest of us," Bessie remarked.

"We haven't had an opportunity for everyone to get acquainted," Andrew replied. "All of our meetings have been about cases. Dinner tonight will mostly be social, though."

"I can't stay for long," Hugh warned him. "My late shift starts at seven."

Bessie finished the last of her hot chocolate as the others gathered their things and left. As Andrew stood up, Hugh shouldered his backpack and headed out to the room that Jasper had offered to let him use.

"What shall we do with our afternoon?" Andrew asked Bessie.

"After the last case, we went shopping in Ramsey," she replied. "We were just there, though. What do you want to do?"

"You're welcome to pass the time in our library," Jasper said from the doorway.

"You have a library?" Bessie asked.

"It's something we'd been wanting to do since we bought the place," he told her. "Because it isn't absolutely necessary, it kept getting moved down the list of priorities, but I finally put my foot down and insisted that we at least make a start. It isn't finished, but we're including it in all of our promotional materials now. Come and have a look."

Bessie gathered up her things and eagerly followed Jasper back down to the ground floor. Halfway down the corridor that was full of conference rooms was a door with a small sign that said "Guest Library." Jasper unlocked the door and reached in to turn on a light before he stood back to let Bessie walk in first. Andrew was right behind her.

The room was about the same size as the conference rooms they'd been using for their meetings, but, unlike those rooms, here there were windows, several of them along one wall. The view of the beach and the sea was stunning, and Bessie stared at that for a moment before she looked around the room.

Several large, overstuffed chairs were scattered around the space. There was a fireplace on one wall, and Bessie guessed that it contained a gas fire. Jasper confirmed her suspicions when he flipped a switch and the fire turned on. The remaining two walls were completely covered in bookshelves that ran from floor to ceiling.

"We're going to do our best to fill the shelves," Jasper told her.

At the moment, only a few of the shelves were full, although many others had at least a few books neatly lined up along them.

"It's lovely," Bessie told him. "I feel as if I could spend hours in here, sitting by the fire and watching the sea. Oh, and reading, as well."

He laughed. "We want the space to be somewhere guests can feel comfortable doing just that. They'll be permitted to borrow the books, but not to take them home. Of course, we do expect a few to go missing now and again. We're doing most of our shopping at charity shops and car boot sales."

Bessie nodded. "Are you putting the books into any sort of order?"

"I'm trying, which is why some shelves are full and others have only a book or two on them. I started with books from my own collection that I don't mind sharing, which is why the science fiction and mystery and thriller sections take up so many shelves. Stuart added some biographies and autobiographies, as that's what he prefers to read. Then we went shopping and bought just about every book we found at the charity shops in Ramsey. If you're interested in guidebooks to Australia from the nineteen seventies, we have a large set."

Andrew laughed. "We're going to have to spend an hour or two in here, just looking to see what you have."

"You're more than welcome to visit any time. While it's technically for guests, you're both customers of the hotel," Jasper told him.

Bessie looked at Andrew. "We could just stay here until time for dinner," she suggested.

"Maybe I could leave you here for a short while. I want to check my emails one more time. It's just possible that Jeff has heard more from Berlin."

"That's fine with me," Bessie said quickly. While she enjoyed Andrew's company, she'd be perfectly happy on her own in the library.

When he returned just before six, Bessie was lost in a mystery by an author she'd never read before. She jumped as Andrew walked into the room.

"Good book?" he asked.

"It's not the best mystery I've ever read, but I've fallen in love with the characters. I'm just hoping it's the first in a series so that I can read more about them."

At six, she slid a bookmark into the book and then slipped it into her bag. "I did check with Jasper," she told Andrew. "He said I could borrow as many books as I want."

"I wasn't going to accuse you of stealing it," he laughed.

When they reached the restaurant, Hugh was already at the table, with his dinner in front of him. "I hope you don't mind," he said when they joined him.

"Not at all. We know you have to go," Andrew replied.

The others trickled in over the next five minutes. Harry was the last to arrive.

"So, a bit of news," Andrew began. He stopped when something caught his eye.

Bessie followed his gaze and frowned. *What is Dan Ross doing here?*

Dan seemed to be trying to hide, crouching halfway behind a large white pillar, but his dark jacket and trousers only made him stand out against it. As Bessie watched, the restaurant's assistant manager went over and spoke to Dan. After a short conversation, the woman led Dan to a table on the opposite side of the room.

"He's desperate to work out what we're doing," Doona said.

"He shouldn't be able to hear us from there, at least," Bessie replied.

"Jeff spoke to the police in Berlin today," Andrew said after a moment. "They've been speaking with Anja. Leon recently gave her one of his old computers when hers stopped working. She's offered to let the police experts take a look at it to see if they can find anything of interest on it."

"He'll have completely wiped the hard drive before he gave it to her," Charles predicted.

"And it might not be the computer he used for anything related to the case, but it's somewhere else to look for evidence," Andrew said. "And now, we need to stop talking about the case and spend some time getting to know one another better."

An awkward silence descended on the table. While the waiter brought their drinks and took their order, Bessie tried to think of something the group could discuss. As he walked away, she smiled at everyone.

"I spent some time in the library here today. What kinds of books does everyone enjoy?"

Harry and Charles exchanged glances, but after a moment, Harry cleared his throat.

"I like reading true crime stories. I can't stand police procedurals, as they always get things wrong," he said.

"You've been reading the wrong ones," Andrew told him. "There are a few very good authors out there who used to be with the police. They don't often get things wrong."

They were still discussing books when Hugh had to leave. He gave Bessie a hug before he headed out, carrying his backpack full of books. An hour later, everyone was just finishing their puddings, and the conversation was beginning to lag.

"Good evening," Dan Ross said as he approached the table. "You seem to have been having a very lively discussion over here. It made me feel quite lonely on my own."

Doona laughed. "You need to make some friends," she suggested.

Dan nodded. "I work too hard," he said.

Bessie felt sorry for him for a moment, but it didn't last long.

"I expect this is something of a working holiday for the police inspectors among you," Dan said, his gaze moving from Harry to Charles to Andrew.

"It's a lovely island," Harry replied. "And the Seaview is delightful."

Bessie nearly choked on her tea. Delightful wasn't a word she'd expected to hear from Harry. Across the table, Doona turned a laugh into a cough. John leaned over to pat her back, and Bessie suspected that he was using the gesture to hide his own amusement.

"Are you planning on staying here again soon?" Dan asked Harry.

Harry shrugged. "I don't believe my plans are any of your business," he replied, his tone sharp.

"I find it slightly worrying that three senior Scotland Yard police inspectors keep travelling to the island," Dan said defensively. "It suggests that there's some sort of serious criminal investigation going on here. The island's residents have a right to know what is happening." His voice had grown increasingly loud and shrill as he'd spoken.

"The island's residents have nothing to worry about," John replied. "Even senior police inspectors are allowed to have holidays. Besides, all three of the men in question are retired. I don't believe travelling when you're retired actually counts as a holiday, does it?"

He looked at Andrew, who chuckled. Bessie sat back and listened as everyone else began a lively debate as to whether travelling after retirement counted as a holiday or not. After fifteen minutes, Dan finally shook his head.

"You're just wasting my time," he snapped before spinning around and stomping out of the room.

"He wasn't wrong," Harry said as the man disappeared.

Everyone laughed.

"You're very quiet," Andrew said to Bessie as he drove them back to Laxey.

"I was just thinking about Anja," she told him. "The poor woman's first fiancé was murdered, and I believe she's about to learn that her second fiancé killed him. I can't imagine how awful that would be."

"At least they aren't married yet, and don't have children."

Bessie sighed. "As much as solving cases is satisfying, it's also very sad."

He patted her arm. "We're doing what we can to help right wrongs and put guilty people behind bars," he reminded her.

At Treoghe Bwaane, he insisted on having a quick check of the cottage before he left her for the evening.

"We can go sightseeing for the rest of my stay," he told her at the door.

"I'll probably ring Mark and offer to help with Christmas at the Castle a bit earlier than I'd originally planned," she told him.

"I'm happy to help, too," he said. "It sounds as if it should be interesting."

Bessie nodded. "For tonight, though, I'm going to curl up with the book I borrowed from the Seaview and let the nice, kind, and clever young detective solve the murder and make everything right again."

Andrew grinned at her. "Fictional worlds are so much better than the real one."

* * *

TWO WEEKS LATER, as Bessie was trying to decide what to make for dinner, the telephone rang.

"I just wanted to share an update with you on Paul Bernhard's murder," Andrew told her. "I'm going to send everyone else in the unit an email."

"And I don't have a computer yet."

"Exactly," Andrew laughed. "We should think about going computer shopping for you, though. I think you'd find having one very helpful."

"I'll think about it. But what have you learned? Has Leon been arrested?"

"The experts were able to find a great deal on the computer that Leon had given Anja, including copies of all of the correspondence that was meant to have taken place between Paul and Maria. When the police confronted Leon with what they'd found, he confessed to the murder, although he claimed that he'd killed Paul in self-defense after they'd argued. The police are still sorting through it all, but it appears that he rang Paul and told him he was in trouble and needed help. Paul was kind enough to drop everything and fly to the US on short notice to help his friend."

"And then Leon killed him," Bessie said flatly.

"According to Leon, he asked Paul to meet him at the apartment building because he was considering buying a flat in the building. He claims that the doors were open and that they simply walked inside. Once in the model apartment, they began to argue over Anja and at some point, according to Leon, Paul tried to punch him. From there, Leon claims he was simply defending himself," Andrew told her.

"Where does Maria fit into Leon's story, then?" Bessie asked.

"Leon told the police that Maria was one of the things that he and Paul had argued about. He claims that Paul had sent him copies of all of the emails and that he was upset that Paul was cheating on Anja but wouldn't end the relationship."

"Which isn't any more believable than anything else he's said."

"No, it's not. So, that's another successful result for our cold case unit. I'm afraid we're going to get too much attention now."

"It's all down to you choosing the right cases for us to consider," Bessie told him.

"I wish I could believe that, but I think it's more to do with my having chosen the right people to be a part of the unit. You've been especially brilliant. Thank you."

Bessie felt herself blushing as she quickly changed the subject.

THE CARTER FILE

AN AUNT BESSIE COLD CASE MYSTERY

Release date: July 16, 2021
Turn the page for a sneak peek.

Julie Carter was celebrating her high school graduation with five friends on a rainy weekend in 1985. Her murder is the third case that Andrew Cheatham presents to his cold case unit. One of the five people at the cottage with Julie killed her, but, more than a decade later, no one has ever been arrested.

Bessie is determined to get justice for poor Julie, but she's also busy with other things. Christmas at the Castle is less than a month away, and her friend, Grace, is worried about a friend of hers who has gone missing.

Can Bessie help Andrew and the others work out what happened in the luxury cottage during graduation weekend? Can she find Grace's friend? And can she talk some sense into Andy Caine, who seems determined to marry the wrong woman?

A SNEAK PEEK AT THE CARTER FILE

AN AUNT BESSIE COLD CASE MYSTERY

Release date: July 16, 2021

Please excuse any typos or minor errors. I have not yet completed final edits on this title.

Chapter One

The knock on the door surprised Elizabeth Cubbon. She wasn't expecting any visitors on the last day of November. It was cold and wet outside the window, and she couldn't imagine that anyone had come to see her to admire her view of the beach, either.

"Harry?" she said questioningly as she opened the door to someone completely unexpected.

"Miss Cubbon, good afternoon," Harry Blake replied. "I hope I'm not interrupting anything important?"

"Call me Bessie," she said automatically as she tried to work out what the man could possibly want.

Harry was a retired Scotland Yard inspector who worked on Andrew Cheatham's cold case unit with Bessie. He was a tall man, with dark hair streaked with grey. His eyes were dark as well and, to Bessie, they seemed to belong to a much older man, one who had seen many horrible things in his lifetime. The pair had barely spoken, though, over the past two months since the unit had begun meeting. Harry lived in London and only came to the island for a week each month for their meetings. He stayed at the Seaview Hotel in Ramsey while he was there and, as far as Bessie had known, he didn't even know where she lived.

Of course, she'd lived on the Isle of Man for a great many years. Nearly anyone on the island could have told Harry where to find "Aunt Bessie's" cottage.

He smiled. "Thank you, Bessie."

"And do come in," she added, realising that he'd been standing in the rain while she'd been lost in thought.

"Thank you again," Harry said. He stepped carefully into the cottage and then slowly looked around the room.

Bessie watched his face as he studied her cosy kitchen. He seemed to be taking in every single detail, and Bessie found herself wondering when she'd last scrubbed the top of her refrigerator. No doubt Harry had catalogued exactly how much dust had gathered there since she'd last cleaned.

"Have a seat," she said after an awkward pause. She waved at the small table in the corner of the room. There were four chairs around it, including the one Bessie had been sitting on when the man had knocked. She'd left her book of logic puzzles open on the table when she'd answered the door.

Harry took a few steps towards the table and then looked back at her. "I've interrupted your logic puzzle," he said. "I am sorry."

She shrugged. "I couldn't work it out anyway. I should just stop when I get about halfway through the book. That's usually where the puzzles begin to get too difficult for me."

"I've never tried them," he said as he dropped into the

chair opposite the one Bessie had been using. "I never seem to have the time."

"I thought you were retired?"

"I am, in theory, but I do quite a lot of consulting work. It keeps me busy, and I still enjoy it. If I'm honest, I miss working."

Thanks to a small inheritance at eighteen, Bessie had never held down a paying job. Over the years, she'd filled her time with a great deal of volunteer work, but the small sum that she was being paid for taking part in the cold case unit was the first time she'd ever received a pay cheque. It was difficult, therefore, for her to understand what Harry missed about working.

"I should think you'd enjoy being able to do whatever you want all the time," she replied as she walked to the sink. "Tea?"

"Tea would be much appreciated, thank you. I've never really had any hobbies. I loved my job and it's pretty much what I want to do all the time," he told her.

While she waited for the kettle to boil, she got down a box of biscuits and arranged some on a plate. After putting that on the table, she added smaller plates for each of them and then made the tea. As she sat down in her chair, she shut the logic puzzle book and pushed it to one side.

"Thank you," Harry said as he took a few biscuits and put them on his plate.

"But what can I do for you?" Bessie asked, feeling as if she'd only just managed to avoid blurting out the question every second since the man had arrived.

"We've considered two cases thus far in the cold case unit," Harry replied after a sip of tea. "And your input has been key to both solutions. I want to get to know you better. I want to learn more about everyone on the team, actually."

"Everyone?" Bessie echoed, not certain what the man was after.

"When we started, Andrew told us to expect that we'd solve about ten per cent of our cases. I thought he was being optimistic. I've been involved in these sorts of units before and we never solved even five per cent of our cases. With this unit, we're two for two, and I want to understand why. You and your friends work well together. I want you to tell me all about all of you."

Bessie took a sip of tea and then slowly ate a biscuit while she tried to think. It wasn't that she didn't want to tell the man about herself and her friends, exactly. She just didn't enjoy feeling as if she didn't have a choice. "I see," she said eventually.

"I know that we all introduced ourselves at the first meeting, but I had other things on my mind at that time and I don't really recall what was said. I've tapped a few sources to get some basic facts, but I want to learn more. Obviously, how much you tell me is entirely up to you," Harry added. "I'd love to hear more about the island, as well. I'd never been here before the first meeting and I'm surprised by how lovely it is, actually."

"I'm glad you feel that way. When Andrew first told me about the cold case unit and mentioned that you and Charles were going to be a part of it, he suggested that he might meet with you two in London and the rest of us here. I think it works better if we're all together, though."

Harry nodded. "I may not come over every month, but for now I've been able to fit the meetings into my schedule. It helps that we're meeting early this month. Things get crazy around Christmas."

"Indeed. I'm involved with a charity fundraiser that starts in the middle of the month. I'm not certain that I'd be able to attend the meetings if they were much later in

December. And I've a wedding to go to at the end of the month, as well."

"What sort of charity fundraiser?"

"It's called Christmas at the Castle. It's held at Castle Rushen in Castletown. Different charities from around the island each decorate a room in the castle for Christmas and then the public can buy tickets to see the beautiful decorations. They get to vote for their favourites, and all of the charities share the proceeds from ticket sales and also from an auction on the last evening," Bessie explained.

"I saw the castle from the outside when I drove around the island, but I haven't visited it properly. It looked to be a substantial medieval fortress."

"It is, indeed. It was a prison for many years and now it's a museum, although some parts are still used for other things."

"There's also a castle in Peel, although that one didn't look as well maintained."

Bessie laughed. "Peel Castle is mostly in ruins. There are a few standing structures, but the entire site is a heritage site. I highly recommend a visit to both castles, though, if you can find the time."

Harry glanced out the window at the heavy rain. "Maybe in the spring," he told her.

"Actually, both castles are shut at the moment, anyway, although I reckon I could get someone to show you around if you really wanted to see them now."

"You have connections with whoever owns the castles?"

"They're owned by Manx National Heritage, and I've done volunteer work with them for many years."

"How many years?"

Bessie flushed. "Since it was founded in the early fifties, actually."

"And you've lived on the island for your entire life?"

"My entire adult life, yes, but not my entire life," Bessie

replied. She took a sip of tea while she considered how much she wanted to tell the man. Her life story was well known on the island, of course. Harry could ask just about anyone about her and probably be told more than she'd really care for him to know. Some of would be untrue, of course, but the island's gossips didn't worry much about keeping the facts straight, not if some embellishments made for a better story.

She sighed. "I was born on the island, but my parents decided to move to America when I was two. We settled near Cleveland, Ohio, where other family members were already living. When I was seventeen, they decided that we were going to move back."

"That must have been difficult for you. Surely, you didn't remember anything about the island. Ohio was all that you'd ever known."

"That's very true," Bessie replied. "I didn't want to leave the US. It was home for me, and I'd also met a man, one that I was convinced was the only man in the world for me."

"Since you're here, I'm going to guess that your parents wouldn't let you stay behind in the US."

"No, they would not. My older sister was engaged to a man she'd been seeing for several years. They got married very quickly and she stayed in the US with him. My parents refused to give me permission to marry Matthew Saunders, the man I loved. I was only seventeen and they wouldn't hear of my staying behind with a man they barely knew."

"So they dragged you back to the island?"

"They did," Bessie agreed. She hesitated for a moment and then decided that she might as well tell him the rest of the story. "Matthew wrote to me a short while later to tell me that he was coming to get me. Unfortunately, he didn't survive the sea journey. He passed away shortly before the ship docked in Liverpool," she said. Even after so many years,

Bessie had to blink several times and swallow hard to keep her emotions in check.

"I'm sorry," Harry said after a moment.

"It was a long time ago. Matthew left me all of his worldly goods. I had enough money to buy this cottage, with a bit left over. My very clever advocate invested the extra money on my behalf and, thanks to him, I've lived off of that money ever since."

"He must have been very clever."

She nodded. For many years, she'd lived life expecting to be told at any time that the money had run out, but instead, her investments had continued to grow. After living very frugally for such a long time, she was now at a point in her life where she could truly spoil herself. For Bessie, that meant buying hardcover books instead of waiting for the paperback versions to be released. Beyond that, she was quite content in her little cottage by the sea, and she knew that one day her relatives in America would be pleasantly surprised by the size of their inheritance from her.

"So you bought this cottage when you were eighteen?" Harry asked, looking around the kitchen again.

"I did. I've had two extensions added, and I had the kitchen remodelled in the late fifties. I can't imagine that I'll do anything further with it now that I've settled into middle age."

Harry stared at her for a moment and then nodded very slowly. "I wasn't going to ask your age," he said.

"It's none of your business," she replied tartly. "I stopped keeping track of my age when I got my free bus pass. When I get a birthday card from the Queen, well, then I'll know I've hit one hundred, but until then, I'm not counting."

"That's very wise, actually. And you've never been married?"

"There was another man who once suggested that we

might marry, but I turned him down. He lived in Australia and I wasn't interested in leaving the island."

Harry nodded. "Tell me about your friends," he requested. "The ones in the cold case unit, I mean. I'm not expecting you to tell me their deepest, darkest secrets, but I really want to hear how you all became friends. You don't seem to have much in common."

Bessie nodded. "We don't, really, I suppose. But I don't even know where to start." She picked up her teacup and frowned at it. "I need more tea," she told Harry. After she'd poured them each a second cup of tea and added a few more biscuits to the plate, she sat back down.

"Let's start with Hugh. I've known him the longest," she suggested.

"Constable Hugh Watterson, mid-twenties, married to Grace, one child, a daughter called Alice," Harry said.

"His daughter is Aalish," Bessie corrected him.

"Can you spell that for me?"

Bessie laughed and complied. "It's the Manx form of Alice, so you weren't too far off," she added.

"But I was wrong," he said with a frown. "I'm going to have to go back through my notes and see if I got bad information or simply remembered it incorrectly. But you were saying…"

"I've known Hugh since he was a child. Laxey Beach is a popular place for children to play in the summer months. It was even more popular before the holiday cottages were built."

Just past Bessie's cottage was a long row of small holiday cottages. Thomas and Maggie Shimmin had purchased the homes that had been there for decades and then torn them down to make space for their holiday rentals. The beach itself was still open to the public, but in the summer months, when the cottages were full of holidaymakers, there was limited room for Laxey families to come and enjoy the sand and the sea.

"And Hugh used to play on the beach?" Harry asked.

"He spent as much time down here as he could," Bessie replied, remembering the small boy who used to race up and down the sand, seemingly unable to use up all of his energy.

"And do you often speak to the children on the beach?" Harry asked.

"As I've never had children of my own, I've always been something of an honorary aunt to the boys and girls in Laxey," Bessie explained. "Many of them used to enjoy coming to my cottage for biscuits during their time at the beach. Once they became teenagers, they saw my cottage as a safe place where they could come if they were having problems with their parents. I have a spare bedroom and I used to allow boys or girls to spend the night when things were difficult at home."

"You're speaking as if that no longer happens."

Bessie frowned. "In the past three years, I've been involved in a number of murder investigations. Over those years, parents have become increasingly reluctant to allow their children to stay with me. At times I miss having children and teenagers around, but I do enjoy having my cottage all to myself, as well."

"But we were talking about Hugh."

"We were. His parents didn't approve of him joining the police, so he took to spending quite a lot of his time here during his teen years. His parents are both incredibly proud of him now, though, and I know they adore Aalish."

"So you and Hugh have been friends since he was a child."

"I've known him since he was a child. We became friends the first time I stumbled over a dead body. He was first constable on the scene that awful day nearly three years ago."

"How long have you known the others, then?"

"I met Doona Moore nearly five years ago now."

"Ah, Mrs. Moore," he said. "You'll probably tell me that I've something wrong with what I know about her, too. She's in her mid-forties. She's been married twice, divorced once, and widowed once. When her second husband died, he left her a considerable fortune, although she's had some difficulty getting her hands on it due to legal complications. I believe she's wealthy enough now that she's stopped working, although she was formerly a receptionist at the Laxey Constabulary. I also believe that she and John Rockwell are, um, a couple."

"I suppose all of that is correct, although it sounds odd when simply listed in that way. I met Doona at a Manx language class. I was taking it for the third time, but it was her first attempt."

"I understand Celtic languages are very difficult."

"They are, at least for me. I've taken the class multiple times and I still can't say much more than *moghrey mie*."

"Which means?"

"Good morning, and it isn't even morning," Bessie laughed. "Anyway, I met Doona in the class. She'd signed up hoping to meet single men, but she was far and away the youngest person there. Her second marriage was falling apart at that point and I did my best to help her through what was a very difficult time for her."

"And you've been friends ever since," Harry concluded for her.

"We have, through multiple murder investigations, including that of her second husband."

"So when did you meet John Rockwell? I know he's the police inspector in charge of the Laxey Constabulary. He was with the police in Manchester before he moved to the island. He's in his mid-forties and divorced, although his former wife, Susan, passed away nearly a year ago. They had two children, Thomas and Amy, who now live with John. I believe they're both in their teens."

"That's all correct, although I'm not entirely certain that John's wife was actually Susan. I've only every heard her called Sue. Of course, that's a nickname for Susan, but it doesn't have to be."

Harry nodded. "I'll check my sources."

What sources, Bessie wondered. "I met John over that same dead body that I mentioned earlier, the first one that I was unfortunate enough to discover. He was the inspector put in charge of the investigation and, over the years since, we've become friends."

"Interesting," Harry said. "And how did you meet Andrew?"

Bessie smiled. "In the middle of another murder investigation, actually, at a holiday park in the UK. It was Doona's second husband who'd turned up dead. Andrew simply happened to be staying in the cabin next to the one that Doona and I were sharing. We started talking and, eventually, we were able to work together to help the police solve the case."

"And based on that, Andrew invited you to be a part of the cold case unit?"

"We stayed in touch after we'd both returned home. Andrew came to visit some months later and, while he was here, he told me about a cold case. Again we were able to work together to solve the case. According to him, that was where the idea for the cold case unit first arose."

"Really?" Harry glanced at his watch and then got to his feet. "As fascinating as this has been, I'm afraid I have an appointment elsewhere. Thank you very much for your time."

Bessie walked him to the door. "I'll see you at the meeting tomorrow," she said.

"Yes, I'm looking forward to it. Andrew said it's murder again," Harry replied.

Bessie watched as he crossed the small parking area outside of her cottage. His car was the only one there, a small black car with a large orange sticker that identified which hire car company owned it. Harry waved as he drove away.

"But what did he want?" Bessie asked as she cleared away the cups and plates. She felt as if she'd told him a great deal about herself and her friends, but the more she thought about it, the more she realised that she'd learned nothing about him. Frowning, she sat back down with her logic puzzle book and pencil. *Tomorrow, when Andrew arrives, I'll ask him about Harry,* she decided.

ALSO BY DIANA XARISSA

The Isle of Man Cozy Mysteries

Aunt Bessie Assumes

Aunt Bessie Believes

Aunt Bessie Considers

Aunt Bessie Decides

Aunt Bessie Enjoys

Aunt Bessie Finds

Aunt Bessie Goes

Aunt Bessie's Holiday

Aunt Bessie Invites

Aunt Bessie Joins

Aunt Bessie Knows

Aunt Bessie Likes

Aunt Bessie Meets

Aunt Bessie Needs

Aunt Bessie Observes

Aunt Bessie Provides

Aunt Bessie Questions

Aunt Bessie Remembers

Aunt Bessie Solves

Aunt Bessie Tries

Aunt Bessie Understands

Aunt Bessie Volunteers

Aunt Bessie Wonders

Aunt Bessie's X-Ray

Aunt Bessie Yearns

Aunt Bessie Zeroes In

The Aunt Bessie Cold Case Mysteries

The Adams File

The Bernhard File

The Carter File

The Markham Sisters Cozy Mystery Novellas

The Appleton Case

The Bennett Case

The Chalmers Case

The Donaldson Case

The Ellsworth Case

The Fenton Case

The Green Case

The Hampton Case

The Irwin Case

The Jackson Case

The Kingston Case

The Lawley Case

The Moody Case

The Norman Case

The Osborne Case

The Patrone Case

The Quinton Case

The Rhodes Case

The Somerset Case

The Tanner Case

The Underwood Case

The Vernon Case

The Walters Case

The Xanders Case

The Young Case

The Zachery Case

The Janet Markham Bennett Cozy Thriller Series

The Armstrong Assignment

The Blake Assignment

The Isle of Man Ghostly Cozy Mysteries

Arrivals and Arrests

Boats and Bad Guys

Cars and Cold Cases

Dogs and Danger

Encounters and Enemies

Friends and Frauds

Guests and Guilt

Hop-tu-Naa and Homicide

Invitations and Investigations

Joy and Jealousy

Kittens and Killers

Letters and Lawsuits

Marsupials and Murder

Neighbors and Nightmares

Orchestras and Obsessions

Proposals and Poison

Questions and Quarrels

Roses and Revenge

The Isle of Man Romance Series

Island Escape

Island Inheritance

Island Heritage

Island Christmas

The Later in Life Love Stories

Second Chances

Second Act

Second Thoughts

Second Degree

Second Best

Second Nature

ABOUT THE AUTHOR

Diana started self-publishing in 2013 and she is thrilled to have found readers for the stories that she creates. She spent her childhood and teens years wearing out her library card on a regular basis and has always enjoyed getting lost in fictional worlds.

She was born and raised in Erie, Pennsylvania, and studied history at Allegheny College in Meadville, Pennsylvania. After years working in college administration in both Erie and Washington, DC, Diana moved to the UK following her marriage.

While living on the Isle of Man, Diana had an opportunity to earn a master's degree in Manx Studies, focusing on the fascinating history of the island. Eventually, she and her husband and their two children relocated to the US, where they are now settled in the Buffalo, New York, area.

She also writes mystery/thrillers set in the not-too-distant future as Diana X. Dunn and Middle Grade and Young Adult fiction as D.X. Dunn.

Diana is always happy to hear from readers. You can write to her at:

Diana Xarissa Dunn
PO Box 72

Clarence, NY 14031.

Find Diana at: DianaXarissa.com
E-mail: Diana@dianaxarissa.com

Printed in France by Amazon
Brétigny-sur-Orge, FR